Blood Line

Blood Line

Stories of Fathers and Sons

David Quammen

Johnson Books
Boulder

First Johnson Books Edition 2000
Copyright © 1988 by David Quammen

Grateful acknowledgment is made to the editors of *TriQuarterly*, in which two of these stories, in different form, first appeared. "Walking Out" appeared in 1980, and "Nathan's Rime" appeared in 1982.

Author's Note: Concerning "Uriah's Letter": In addition to the debt that will be most obvious, I am also deeply beholden to Shelby Foote.

Published by Johnson Books, a division of Johnson Publishing Company, 1880 South 57th Court, Boulder, Colorado 80301.
E-mail: books@jpcolorado.com

9   8   7   6   5   4   3   2   1

Cover design by Debra B. Topping
Cover illustration by Adam DeKraker

Library of Congress Cataloging-in-Publication Data
Quammen, David, 1948-
  Blood line: stories of fathers and sons / David Quammen.
    p.   cm.
  ISBN 1-55566-272-2 (pbk.: alk. paper)
  1. Fathers and sons—Fiction. 2. Domestic fiction, American. I. Title.
PS3567.U25 B55 2000
813'.54—dc21   00-042833

Printed in the United States by
Johnson Printing
1880 South 57th Court
Boulder, Colorado 80301

♻ Printed on recycled paper with soy ink

to
Albert E. Quammen
1877 – 1954

Contents

ℳ Walking Out ℳ

AS THE TRAIN ROCKED DEAD at Livingston he saw the man, in a worn khaki shirt with button flaps buttoned, arms crossed. The boy's hand sprang up by reflex, and his face broke into a smile. The man smiled back gravely, and nodded. He did not otherwise move. The boy turned from the window and, with the awesome deliberateness of a fat child harboring reluctance, began struggling to pull down his bag. His father would wait on the platform. First sight of him had reminded the boy that nothing was simple enough now for hurrying.

They drove in the old open Willys toward the cabin beyond town. The windshield of the Willys was up, but the fine cold sharp rain came into their faces, and the boy could not raise his eyes to look at the road. He wore a rain parka his father had handed him at the station. The man, protected by only the khaki, held his lips strung in a firm silent line that seemed more grin than wince. Riding through town in the cold rain, open topped and jaunty, getting drenched as though by necessity, was—the boy understood vaguely— somehow in the spirit of this season.

"We have a moose tag," his father shouted.

The boy said nothing. He refused to care what it meant, that they had a moose tag.

"I've got one picked out. A bull. I've stalked him for two

weeks. Up in the Crazies. When we get to the cabin, we'll build a good roaring fire." With only the charade of a pause, he added, "Your mother." It was said like a question. The boy waited. "How is she?"

"All right, I guess." Over the jeep's howl, with the wind stealing his voice, the boy too had to shout.

"Are you friends with her?"

"I guess so."

"Is she still a beautiful lady?"

"I don't know. I guess so. I don't know that."

"You must know that. Is she starting to get wrinkled like me? Does she seem worried and sad? Or is she just still a fine beautiful lady? You must know that."

"She's still a beautiful lady, I guess."

"Did she tell you any messages for me?"

"She said ... she said I should give you her love," the boy lied, impulsively and clumsily. He was at once embarrassed that he had done it.

"Oh," his father said. "Thank you, David."

They reached the cabin on a mile of dirt road winding through meadow to a spruce grove. Inside, the boy was enwrapped in the strong syncretic smell of all seasonal mountain cabins: pine resin and insect repellent and a mustiness suggesting damp bathing trunks stored in a drawer. There were yellow pine floors and rope-work throw rugs and a bead curtain to the bedroom and a cast-iron cook stove with none of the lids or handles missing and a pump in the kitchen sink and old issues of *Field and Stream*, and on the mantel above where a fire now finally burned was a picture of the boy's grandfather, the railroad telegrapher, who had once owned the cabin. The boy's father cooked a dinner of fried ham, and though the boy did not like ham he had expected his father to cook canned stew or Spam, so he said nothing.

His father asked him about school and the boy talked and his father seemed to be interested. Warm and dry, the boy began to feel safe from his own anguish. Then his father said:

"We'll leave tomorrow around ten."

Last year on the boy's visit they had hunted birds. They had lived in the cabin for six nights, and each day they had hunted pheasant in the wheat stubble, or blue grouse in the woods, or ducks along the irrigation sloughs. The boy had been wet and cold and miserable at times, but each evening they returned to the cabin and to the boy's suitcase of dry clothes. They had eaten hot food cooked on a stove, and had smelled the cabin smell, and had slept together in a bed. In six days of hunting, the boy had not managed to kill a single bird. Yet last year he had known that, at least once a day, he would be comfortable, if not happy. This year his father planned that he should not even be comfortable. He had said in his last letter to Evergreen Park, before the boy left Chicago but when it was too late for him not to leave, that he would take the boy camping in the mountains, after big game. He had pretended to believe that the boy would be glad.

Last year his father had given him a 16-gauge over-and-under, and on the first morning they had practiced until the boy's shoulder was bruised. He had never before fired a gun. He hit a few coffee cans. Then they walked in the woods after blue grouse, and his father turned quickly, and the boy heard a rustle, and his father fired, and a blue grouse was dead in the bushes.

"Like that," his father said. "They're stupid, and slow. Not like a duck."

His father killed four blue grouse in five shots before he began to touch the boy's elbow and whisper, "There, David," instead of shooting. But the woods were thick and confused with bare alder bushes and everything was the same color and the blue grouse were faster than the boy could lift the gun. The ducks and pheasants were faster than the blue grouse. The boy's aim was not good. Sometimes he fired with his eyes closed, to see if it made any difference. It did not. So he gave up. Long before his father let him stop shooting, the boy had given up.

"It's hard, I know," his father said. "And then it gets easier. Eventually, you'll hit your first bird. You will. Then all of a sudden it gets very easy. But you have to keep trying. Don't close your eyes, David." The boy knew his father was lying. His father often said things were easy, when the boy knew they were not.

Then the boy hit his first grouse. The boy did not know whether he had hit it or not, but his father said that he had. He had hit it in the wing, and it faltered, and dropped. They went to the spot and searched the brush and the ground for an hour. Even his father could not find the crippled grouse, and they did not have a dog. The boy's father would not own a hunting dog. He had said that, since he was already alone, he did not want to give that much love to a creature who would only live fourteen or fifteen years. The bird must have run off and hidden itself to die, his father said.

The boy was disappointed at not finding the grouse. But his father, the boy could see, was even more disappointed. An hour seemed a very long time to keep looking.

"Just too bad we couldn't find that blue grouse you killed," his father had said at the station, when the boy left, and the boy was embarrassed. He understood how his father felt. So he had agreed to come back for hunting this year. His father did not mean to make everything difficult for the boy. He couldn't help it.

Now a deer or a moose would be a much bigger target than a blue grouse. But a deer is not slow, the boy knew, and is probably not stupid, he thought. He knew nothing about a moose except that it was stupid-looking. The boy wished again that they could have found the blue grouse he may have wounded last year, found it dead, and eaten it roasted in butter as they had the birds his father killed. That would have made a great difference to the boy now.

They would leave around ten the next day for the Crazy Mountains. The boy slept on the far edge of the bed, and did not let himself touch up against his father's warm body.

Then there was nothing, then more cold, and then the faint steady gray light of November dawn. The boy's father was up, and the stove was already making its warm noises. After breakfast they sighted in the boy's gun. They set up coffee cans on a fence in the meadow, and the boy hit a few. The rain had paused, so the boy was only drenched from the thighs down.

This year his father gave him a different gun. It was a lever-action Winchester .30-30, with open sights. It was a simple gun. It was older than the over-and-under, and it was probably a better gun, the boy could see, and it was certainly heavier and more powerful. This was just like the rifle with which he had killed his own first moose, when he was thirteen, the boy's father said. This was not the same rifle, but it was just like it. The boy's grandfather, the railroad telegrapher, had given him that gun. A boy should learn how to shoot with open sights, his father said, before he learns to depend on a telescope.

The Willys was loaded and moving by ten minutes to ten. For three hours they drove, through Big Timber, and then north on the highway, and then back west again on a logging road that took them winding and bouncing higher into the mountains. Thick cottony streaks of white cloud hung in among the mountain-top trees, light and dense dollops against the bulking sharp dark olive, as though in a black-

and-white photograph. They followed the gravel road for an hour, and the boy thought they would soon have a flat tire or break an axle. If they had a flat, the boy knew, his father would only change it and drive on until they had the second, farther from the highway. Finally they crossed a creek and his father plunged the Willys off into a bed of weeds.

His father said, "Here."

The boy said, "Where?"

"Up that little drainage. At the head of the creek."

"How far is it?"

"Two or three miles."

"Is that where you saw the moose?"

"No. That's where I saw the sheepman's hut. The moose is farther. On top."

"Are we going to sleep in a hut? I thought we were going to sleep in a tent."

"No. Why should we carry a tent up there when we have a perfectly good hut?"

The boy couldn't answer that question. He thought now that this might be the time when he would cry. He had known it was coming.

"I don't much want to sleep in a hut," he said, and his voice broke with the simple honesty of it, and his eyes glazed. He held his mouth tight against the trembling.

As though something had broken in him too, the boy's father laid his forehead down on the steering wheel, against his knuckles. For a moment he remained bowed, breathing exhaustedly. But he looked up again before speaking.

"Well, we don't have to, David."

The boy said nothing.

"It's an old sheepman's hut made of logs, and it's near where we're going to hunt, and we can fix it dry and good. I thought you might like that. I thought it might be more fun

6

than a tent. But we don't have to do it. We can drive back to
Big Timber and buy a tent, or we can drive back to the cabin
and hunt birds, like last year. Whatever you want to do. You
have to forgive me the kind of ideas I get. I hope you will. We
don't have to do anything that you don't want to do."

"No," the boy said. "I want to."

"Are you sure?"

"No," the boy said. "But I just want to."

They bushwhacked along the creek, treading a thick soft
mixture of moss and humus and needles, climbing upward
through brush. Then the brush thinned and they were ascending an open creek bottom, thirty yards wide, darkened
by fir and cedar. Farther, and they struck a trail, which led
them upward along the creek. Farther still, and the trail received a branch, then another, then forked.

"Who made this trail? Did the sheepman?"

"No," his father said. "Deer and elk."

Gradually the creek's little canyon narrowed, steep wooded
shoulders funneling closer on each side. For a while the game
trails forked and converged like a maze, but soon again there
were only two branches, and finally one, heavily worn. It
dodged through alder and willow, skirting tangles of browned
raspberry, so that the boy and his father could never see more
than twenty feet ahead. When they stopped to rest, the boy's
father unstrapped the .270 from his pack and loaded it.

"We have to be careful now," he explained. "We may surprise a bear."

Under the cedars, the creek bottom held a cool dampness
that seemed to be stored from one winter to the next. The boy
began at once to feel chilled. He put on his jacket, and they
continued climbing. Soon he was sweating again in the cold.

On a small flat where the alder drew back from the creek,
the hut was built into one bank of the canyon, with the sod

of the hillside lapping out over its roof. The door was a low dark opening. Forty or fifty years ago, the boy's father explained, this hut had been built and used by a Basque shepherd. At that time there had been many Basques in Montana, and they had run sheep all across this ridge of the Crazies. His father forgot to explain what a Basque was, and the boy didn't remind him.

They built a fire. His father had brought sirloin steaks and an onion for dinner, and the boy was happy with him about that. As they ate, it grew dark, but the boy and his father had stocked a large comforting pile of naked deadfall. In the darkness, by firelight, his father made chocolate pudding. The pudding had been his father's surprise. The boy sat on a piece of canvas and added logs to the fire while his father drank coffee. Sparks rose on the heat and the boy watched them climb toward the cedar limbs and the black pools of sky. The pudding did not set.

"Do you remember your grandfather, David?"

"Yes," the boy said, and wished it were true. He remembered a funeral when he was three.

"Your grandfather brought me up on this mountain when I was seventeen. That was the last year he hunted." The boy knew what sort of thoughts his father was having. But he knew also that his own home was in Evergreen Park, and that he was another man's boy now, with another man's name, though this indeed was his father. "Your grandfather was fifty years older than me."

The boy said nothing.

"And I'm thirty-four years older than you."

"And I'm only eleven," the boy cautioned him.

"Yes," said his father. "And someday you'll have a son and you'll be forty years older than him, and you'll want so badly for him to know who you are that you could cry."

The boy was embarrassed.

"And that's called the cycle of life's infinite wisdom," his father said, and laughed at himself unpleasantly.

"Why didn't he?" the boy asked, to escape the focus of his father's rumination.

"Why didn't who what?"

"Why was it the last year he hunted?"

"He was sixty-seven years old," his father said. "But that wasn't the reason. Because he was still walking to work at the railroad office in Big Timber when he was seventy-five. I don't know. We took a bull elk and a goat that year, I remember. The goat was during spring season and every inch of its hide was covered with ticks. I carried it down whole and after a mile I was covered with ticks too. I never shot another goat. I don't know why he quit. He still went out after birds in the wheat stubble, by himself. So it's not true that he stopped hunting completely. He stopped hunting with me. And he stopped killing. Once in every five or six times he would bring back a pheasant, if it seemed like a particularly good autumn night to have pheasant for supper. Usually he just went out and missed every shot on purpose. There were plenty of birds in the fields where he was walking, and your grandmother or I would hear his gun fire, at least once. But I guess when a man feels himself getting old, almost as old as he thinks he will ever be, he doesn't much want to be killing things anymore. I guess you might have to kill one bird in every ten or twenty, or the pheasants might lose their respect for you. They might tame out. Your grandfather had no desire to live among tame pheasants, I'm sure. But I suppose you would get a little reluctant, when you came to be seventy, about doing your duty toward keeping them wild. And he would not hunt with me anymore then, not even pheasants, not even to miss them. He said it was because he didn't trust himself with a partner, now that his hands were unsteady. But his hands were still steady. He said it was because I was too good. That he had taught me as well as he knew how, and that all I could learn from him now would be the bad habits of age, and those I would find for myself, in my turn. He never did tell me the real reason."

"What did he die of?"

"He was eighty-seven then," said his father. "Christ. He was tired."

The boy's question had been a disruption. His father was silent. Then he shook his head, and poured himself the remaining coffee. He did not like to think of the boy's grandfather as an eighty-seven-year-old man, the boy understood. As long as his grandfather was dead anyway, his father preferred thinking of him younger.

"I remember when I got my first moose," he said. "I was thirteen. I had never shot anything bigger than an owl. And I caught holy hell for killing that owl. I had my Winchester .30-30, like the one you're using. He gave it to me that year, at the start of the season. It was an old-looking gun even then. I don't know where he got it. We had a moose that he had stalked the year before, in a long swampy cottonwood flat along the Yellowstone River. It was a big cow, and this year she had a calf.

"We went there on the first day of the season and every hunting day for a week, and hunted down the length of that river flat, spaced apart about twenty yards, and came out at the bottom end. We saw fresh tracks every day, but we never got a look at that moose and the calf. It was only a matter of time, my father told me, before we would jump her. Then that Sunday we drove out and before he had the truck parked my hands were shaking. I knew it was that day. There was no reason why, yet I had such a sure feeling it was that day, my hands had begun shaking. He noticed, and he said: 'Don't worry.'

"I said: 'I'm fine.' And my voice was steady. It was just my hands.

" 'I can see that,' he said. 'But you'll do what you need to do.'

" 'Yessir,' I said. 'Let's go hunting.'

"That day he put me up at the head end of our cottonwood flat and said he would walk down along the river bank to the bottom, and then turn in. We would come at the moose from both ends and meet in the middle and I should please not shoot my father when he came in sight. I should try to remember, he said, that he was the uglier one, in the orange hat. The shaking had left me as soon as we started walking, holding our guns. I remember it all. Before he went off I said: 'What does a moose look like?'

" 'What the hell do you mean, what does a moose look like?'

" 'Yes, I know,' I said. 'I mean, what is he gonna do when I see him? When he sees me. What color is he? What kind of thing is he gonna do?'

"And he said: 'All right. She will be black. She will be almost pitch black. She will not look to you very much bigger than our pickup. She is going to be stupid. She will let you get close. Slide right up to within thirty or forty yards if you can and set yourself up for a good shot. She will probably not see you, and if she does, she will probably not care. If you miss the first time, which you have every right to do, I don't care how close you get, if you miss the first time, she may even give you another. If you catch her attention, she may bolt off to me or she may charge you. Watch out for the calf when you come up on her. Worry her over the calf, and she will be mad. If she charges you, stand where you are and squeeze off another and then jump the hell out of the way. We probably won't even see her. All right?'

"I had walked about three hundred yards before I saw

what I thought was a Holstein. It was off to my left, away from the river, and I looked over there and saw black and white and kept walking till I was just about past it. There were cattle pastured along in that flat but they would have been beef cattle, Herefords, brown and white like a deer. I didn't think about that. I went on looking everywhere else until I glanced over again when I was abreast and saw I was walking along sixty yards from a grazing moose. I stopped. My heart started pumping so hard that it seemed like I might black out, and I didn't know what was going to happen. I thought the moose would take care of that. Nothing happened.

"Next thing I was running. Running flat out as fast as I could, bent over double like a soldier would do in the field, running as fast but as quietly as I could. Running right at that moose. I remember clearly that I was not thinking anything at all, not for those first seconds. My body just started to run. I never thought, Now I'll scoot up to within thirty yards of her. I was just charging blind, like a moose or a sow grizzly is liable to charge you if you get her mad or confused. Who knows what I would have done. I wanted a moose pretty badly, I thought. I might have galloped right up to within five yards before I leveled, if it hadn't been for that spring creek.

"I didn't see it till I was in the air. I came up a little hillock and jumped, and then it was too late. The hillock turned out to be one bank of a spring-fed pasture seepage, about fifteen feet wide. I landed up to my thighs in mud. It was a prime cattle wallow, right where I had jumped. I must have spent five minutes sweating my legs out of that muck, I was furious with myself, and I was sure the moose would be gone. But the moose was still grazing the same three feet of grass. And by that time I had some of my sense back.

"I climbed the far bank of the mud hole and lay up along the rise where I could steady my aim on the ground. From there I had an open shot of less than forty yards, but the moose was now facing me head on, so I would probably either kill her clean or miss her altogether. My hands started shaking again. I tried to line up the bead and it was ridiculous. My rifle was waving all over that end of the woods. For ten minutes I lay there struggling to control my aim, squeezing the rifle tighter and tighter and taking deeper breaths and holding them longer. Finally I did a smart thing. I set the rifle down. I rolled over on my back and rubbed my eyes and discovered that I was exhausted. I got my breath settled back down in rhythm again. If I could just take that moose, I thought, I was not going to want anything else for a year. But I knew I was not going to do it unless I could get my hands to obey me, no matter how close I was. I tried it again. I remembered to keep breathing easy and low and it was a little better but the rifle was still moving everywhere. When it seemed like the trembling was about to start getting worse all over again I waited till the sights next crossed the moose and jerked off a shot. I missed. The moose didn't even look up.

"Now I was calmer. I had heard the gun fire once, and I knew my father had heard it, and I knew the moose would only give me one more. I realized that there was a good chance I would not get this moose at all, so I was more serious, and humble. This time I squeezed. I knocked a piece off her right antler and before I thought to wonder why a female should have any antlers to get shot at she raised her head up and gave a honk like eleven elephants in a circus-train fire. She started to run.

"I got off my belly and dropped the gun and turned around and jumped right back down into that mud. I was still stuck there when I heard her crash by on her way to the river, and then my father's shot.

"But I had wallowed myself out again, and got my rifle up

off the ground, by the time he found me, thank God. He took a look at my clothes and said:

"'Tried to burrow up under him, did you?'

"'No sir. I heard you fire once. Did you get her?'

"'Him. That was no cow and calf. That was a bull. No. No more than you.'

"He had been at the river edge about a hundred yards downstream from where the bull broke out. He took his shot while the bull was crossing the gravel bed and the shallows. The moose clambered right out into midstream of the Yellowstone and started swimming for his life. But the current along there was heavy. So the moose was swept down abreast with my father before he got halfway across toward the opposite shore. My father sighted on him as he rafted by, dog-paddling frantically and staying afloat and inching slowly away. The moose turned and looked at him, my father said. He had a chunk broken out of one antler and it was dangling down by a few fibers and he looked terrified. He was not more than twenty yards offshore by then and he could see my father and the raised rifle. My father said he had never seen more personality come into the face of a wild animal. All right, my father said the moose told him, Do what you will do. They both knew the moose was helpless. They both also knew this: my father could kill the moose, but he couldn't have him. The Yellowstone River would have him. My father lowered the gun. When he did, my father claimed, the moose turned his head forward again and went on swimming harder than ever. So that wasn't the day I shot mine.

"I shot mine the next Saturday. We went back to the cottonwood flat and split again and I walked up to within thirty yards of the cow and her calf. I made a standing shot, and killed the cow with one bullet breaking her spine. She was drinking, broadside to me. She dropped dead on the spot.

The calf didn't move. He stood over the dead cow, stupid, wondering what in the world to do.

"The calf was as big as a four-point buck. When my father came up, he found me with tears flooding all over my face, screaming at the calf and trying to shoo him away. I was pushing against his flanks and swatting him and shouting at him to run off. At the sight of my father, he finally bolted.

"I had shot down the cow while she stood in the same spring seep where I had been stuck. Her quarters weighed out to eight hundred pounds and we couldn't budge her. We had to clean her and quarter her right there in the water and mud."

His father checked the tin pot again, to be sure there was no more coffee.

"Why did you tell me that story?" the boy said. "Now I don't want to shoot a moose either."

"I know," said his father. "And when you do, I hope you'll be sad too. But the other thing about a moose is, she makes eight hundred pounds of delicious meat. In fact, David, that's what we had for supper."

Through the night the boy was never quite warm. He slept on his side with his knees drawn up, and this was uncomfortable but his body seemed to demand it for warmth. The hard cold mountain earth pressed upward through the mat of fir boughs his father had laid, and drew heat from the boy's body like a pallet of leeches. He clutched the bedroll around his neck and folded the empty part at the bottom back under his legs. Once he woke to a noise. Though his father was sleeping between him and the door of the hut, for a while the boy lay awake, listening worriedly, and then woke again on his back to realize time had passed. He heard droplets begin to hit the canvas his father had spread over the sod roof of the hut. But he remained dry.

He rose to the smell of a fire. The tarp was rigid with sleet and frost. The firewood and knapsacks were frosted. It was that gray time of dawn before any blue and, through the branches above, the boy was unable to tell whether the sky was murky or clear. Delicate sheet ice hung on everything, but there was no wetness. The rain seemed to have been hushed by the cold.

"What time is it?"

"Early yet."

"How early?" The boy was thinking about the cold at home as he waited outside on 96th Street for his school bus. That was the cruelest moment of his day, but it seemed a benign and familiar part of him compared to this.

"Early. I don't have a watch. What difference does it make, David?"

"Not any."

After breakfast they began walking up the valley. His father had the .270 and the boy carried the old Winchester .30-30. The walking was not hard, and with this gentle exercise in the cold morning the boy soon felt fresh and fine. Now I'm hunting for moose with my father, he told himself. That's just what I'm doing. Few boys in Evergreen Park had ever been moose hunting with their fathers in Montana, he knew. I'm doing it now, the boy told himself.

Reaching the lip of a high meadow, a mile above the shepherd's hut, they had not seen so much as a magpie.

Before them, across hundreds of yards, opened a smooth lake of tall lifeless grass, browned by September drought and killed by the frosts and beginning to rot with November's rain. The creek was here a deep quiet channel of smooth curves overhung by the grass, with a dark surface like heavy oil. When they had come fifty yards into the meadow, his father turned and pointed out to the boy a large ponderosa pine with a forked crown that marked the head of their creek valley. He showed the boy a small aspen grove midway across the meadow, toward which they were aligning themselves.

"Near the far woods is a beaver pond. The moose waters there. We can wait in the aspens and watch the whole meadow without being seen. If he doesn't come, we'll go up another canyon, and check again on the way back."

For an hour, and another, they waited. The boy sat, and his buttocks drew cold moisture from the ground. He bunched his jacket around him with hands in the pockets. He was patient. His father squatted on his heels like a country man. Periodically, his father rose and inspected the meadow in all directions.

"He comes once in the morning, and again in the evening, I think. It looked from the tracks like he comes at least twice a day. But he may not show up for hours. You can't tell. If you could, it wouldn't be hunting. It would be shopping.

"He may even know that this is the last week of season. He may remember. So he'll be especially on his guard, and go somewhere else to drink. Somewhere less open." They waited in silence.

"But he may not be all that clever," his father added. "He may make a mistake."

The morning passed, and it was noon.

His father stood. He fixed his stare on the distant meadow, and like a retriever did not move. He said: "David."

The boy stood beside him. His father placed a hand on the boy's shoulder. The boy saw a large dark form rolling toward them like a great slug in the grass.

"Is it the moose?"

"No," said his father. "That is a grizzly bear, David. An old male grizzly."

The boy was impressed. He sensed an aura of power and terror and authority about the husky shape, even at two hundred yards.

"Are we going to shoot him?"

"No."

"Why not?"

"We don't have a permit," his father whispered. "And because we don't want to."

The bear plowed on toward the beaver pond for a while, then stopped. It froze in the grass and seemed to be listening. The boy's father added: "That's not hunting for the meat. That's hunting for the fear. I don't need the fear. I've got enough in my life already."

The bear turned and moiled off quickly through the grass. It disappeared back into the far woods.

"He heard us."

"Maybe," the boy's father said. "Let's go have a look at that beaver pond."

A sleek furred body lay low in the water. The boy thought at first it was a large beaver. It was too large. His father moved quickly ahead off the trail and said nothing. The boy saw that his father was not concerned to surprise it.

The carcass was swollen grotesquely with water and putrescence, and coated with glistening blow-flies. His father did not touch it. Four days, his father guessed. He stood up to his knees in the sump. The moose had been shot at least eighteen times with a .22 pistol. One of its eyes had been shot out, and it had been shot twice in the jaw. Both of the quarters on the side that lay upward had been ruined with shots. The boy's father took the trouble of counting the holes in that side of the carcass, and probing one of the slugs out with his knife. It only made him angrier. He flung the lead away.

Nearby in the fresh mud was the lid from a can of wintergreen chewing tobacco.

For the next three hours, with his father withdrawn into a solitary and characteristic bitterness, the boy felt abandoned.

He did not understand why a moose would be slaughtered with a light pistol and left to rot. His father did not bother to explain; like the bear, he seemed to understand it as well as he needed to. They walked on, but they did not really hunt.

They left the meadow for more pine, and now tamarack, naked tamarack, the yellow needles nearly all down and going ginger where they coated the trail. The boy and his father hiked along a level path into another canyon, this one vast at the mouth and narrowing between high ridges of bare rock. They crossed and recrossed the shepherd's creek, which in this canyon was a tumbling free-stone brook. The boy was miserably uneasy because his father had grown so quiet.

The boy's father tortured him when he spoke at the boy obscurely, both of them knowing that the boy could not hope to understand him, and that his father did not really care whether he did. But the boy preferred even that to his silences.

They wandered forward, deeper into the rock canyon, the boy following five yards behind his father, watching the cold, unapproachable rage that shaped the line of his father's shoulders. They climbed over deadfalls blocking the trail, skirted one boulder large as a cabin, and blundered into a garden of nettles that stung them fiercely through their trousers. They saw fresh elk scat, and bear, diarrhetic with late berries. The boy's father eventually grew bored with brooding. He showed the boy how to stalk. Before dusk that day they had shot an elk.

An open and gently sloped hillside, almost a meadow, ran for a quarter mile in quaking aspen, none over fifteen feet tall. The elk was above. The boy's father had the boy brace his gun in the notch of an aspen and gave him the first shot. The boy missed. The elk reeled and bolted down and his father killed it before it made cover. It was a five-point bull.

His father showed the boy how to approach a downed

animal: from behind, so he could not lash out with his hooves. Get hold of his rack, in case he's not dead, the boy's father explained; reach forward and hook your fingers into the nostrils, he said; and then, suddenly, to the boy's utter shock, his father slit the elk's throat. The boy gagged.

They dressed the elk out and dragged it down the hill to the cover of large pines, near the stream. When they quartered the animal tomorrow, his father said, they would want water. They covered the body with fresh branches, and returned to the hut under twilight. The boy's father was satisfied and the boy was relieved. Again that evening, his father talked.

He talked about the former railroad telegrapher of Big Timber, Montana. He told of going to the station at 6:00 A.M. on school days to find the boy's grandfather bent forward and dozing over the key. He told of walking the old man back home for breakfast, and of his predictable insistence, against all fact, that the night had been busy, full of transmissions. He described how the boy's grandfather became subject to chronic, almost narcoleptic drowsiness after the boy's grandmother, still a young middle-aged woman, checked into the hospital for the last time and began dying. Then, until it faded to embers and the embers went gray, the boy's father stared at his memories, in the fire.

That night even the fetal position could not keep the boy warm. He shivered wakefully for hours. He was glad that the following day, though full of walking and butchery and oppressive burdens, would be their last in the woods. He heard nothing. When he woke, through the door of the hut he saw whiteness like bone.

Six inches had fallen, and it was still snowing. The boy stood about in the campsite, amazed. When it snowed three inches in Evergreen Park, the boy would wake before dawn to the hiss of sand trucks and the ratchet of chains. Here there had been no warning. The boy was not much colder than he had been yesterday, and the transformation of the woods seemed mysterious and benign and somehow comic. He thought of Christmas. Then his father barked at him.

His father's mood had also changed, but in a different way; he seemed serious and hurried. As he wiped the breakfast pots clean with snow, he gave the boy orders for other chores. They left camp with two empty pack frames, both rifles, and a handsaw and rope. The boy soon understood why his father felt pressure of time: it took them an hour to climb the mile to the meadow. The snow continued. They did not rest until they reached the aspens.

"I had half a mind at breakfast to let the bull lie and pack us straight down out of here," his father admitted. "Probably smarter and less trouble in the long run. I could have come back on snowshoes next week. But by then it might be three feet deep and starting to drift. We can get two quarters out today. That will make it easier for me later." The boy was surprised by two things: that his father would be so wary in the face of a gentle snowfall and that he himself would have felt disappointed to be taken out of the woods that morning. The air of the meadow teemed with white.

"If it stops soon, we're fine," said his father.

It continued.

The path up the far canyon was hard climbing in eight inches of snow. The boy fell once, filling his collar and sleeves, and the gun-sight put a small gouge in his chin. But he was not discouraged. That night they would be warm and dry at the cabin. A half mile and he came up beside his father, who had stopped to stare down at dark splashes of blood.

Heavy tracks and a dragging belly mark led up to the scramble of deepening red, and away. The tracks were nine inches long and showed claws. The boy's father knelt. As the boy watched, one shining maroon splotch the size of a saucer sank slowly beyond sight into the snow. The blood was warm.

Inspecting the tracks carefully, his father said, "She's got a cub with her."

"What happened?"

"Just a kill. Seems to have been a bird. That's too much blood for a grouse, but I don't see signs of any four-footed creature. Maybe a turkey." He frowned thoughtfully. "A turkey without feathers. I don't know. What I dislike is coming up on her with a cub." He drove a round into the chamber of the .270.

Trailing red smears, the tracks preceded them. Within fifty feet they found the body. It was half-buried. The top of its head had been shorn away, and the cub's brains had been licked out.

His father said "Christ," and plunged off the trail. He snapped at the boy to follow closely.

They made a wide crescent through brush and struck back after a quarter mile. His father slogged ahead in the snow, stopping often to stand holding his gun ready and glancing around while the boy caught up and passed him. The boy was confused. He knew his father was worried, but he did not feel any danger himself. They met the trail again, and went on to the aspen hillside before his father allowed them to rest. The boy spat on the snow. His lungs ached badly.

"Why did she do that?"

"She didn't. Another bear got her cub. A male. Maybe the one we saw yesterday. Then she fought him for the body, and she won. We didn't miss them by much. She may even have been watching. Nothing could put her in a worse frame of mind."

He added: "If we so much as see her, I want you to pick the nearest big tree and start climbing. Don't stop till you're twenty feet off the ground. I'll stay down and decide whether we have to shoot her. Is your rifle cocked?"

"No."

"Cock it, and put on the safety. She may be a black bear and black bears can climb. If she comes up after you, lean down and stick your gun in her mouth and fire. You can't miss."

He cocked the Winchester, as his father had said.

They angled downhill to the stream, and on to the mound of their dead elk. Snow filtered down steadily in purposeful silence. The boy was thirsty. It could not be much below freezing, he was aware, because with the exercise his bare hands were comfortable, even sweating between the fingers.

"Can I get a drink?"

"Yes. Be careful you don't wet your feet. And don't wander anywhere. We're going to get this done quickly."

He walked the few yards, ducked through the brush at streamside, and knelt in the snow to drink. The water was painful to his sinuses and bitterly cold on his hands. Standing again, he noticed an animal body ahead near the stream bank. For a moment he felt sure it was another dead cub. During that moment his father called:

"David! Get up here right now!"

The boy meant to call back. First he stepped closer to turn the cub with his foot. The touch brought it alive. It rose suddenly with a high squealing growl and whirled its head like a snake and snapped. The boy shrieked. The cub had his right hand in its jaws. It would not release.

It thrashed senselessly, working its teeth deeper and tearing flesh with each movement. The boy felt no pain. He knew his hand was being damaged and that realization terrified him and he was desperate to get the hand back before it was ruined. But he was helpless. He sensed the same furious terror racking the cub that he felt in himself, and he screamed at the cub almost reasoningly to let him go. His screams scared the cub more. Its head snatched back and forth. The boy did not think to shout for his father. He did not see him or hear him coming.

His father moved at full stride in a slowed laboring run through the snow, saying nothing and holding the rifle he did not use, crossed the last six feet still gathering speed, and brought his right boot up into the cub's belly. That kick seemed to lift the cub clear of the snow. It opened its jaws to another shrill piggish squeal, and the boy felt dull relief on his hand, as though his father had pressed open the blades of a spring trap with his foot. The cub tumbled once and disappeared over the stream bank, then surfaced downstream, squalling and paddling. The boy looked at his hand and was horrified. He still had no pain, but the hand was unrecognizable. His fingers had been peeled down through the palm like flaps on a banana. Glands at the sides of his jaw threatened that he would vomit, and he might have stood stupidly watching the hand bleed if his father had not grabbed him.

He snatched the boy by the arm and dragged him toward a tree without even looking at the boy's hand. The boy jerked back in angry resistance as though he had been struck. He screamed at his father. He screamed that his hand was cut, believing his father did not know, and as he screamed he began to cry. He began to feel hot throbbing pain. He began to worry about the blood he was losing. He could imagine his blood melting red holes in the snow behind him and he did not want to look. He did not want to do anything until he had taken care of his hand. At that instant he hated his father. But his father was stronger. He all but carried the boy to a tree.

He lifted the boy. In a voice that was quiet and hurried and very unlike the harsh grip with which he had taken the boy's arm, he said:

"Grab hold and climb up a few branches as best you can. Sit on a limb and hold tight and clamp the hand under your other armpit, if you can do that. I'll be right back to you. Hold tight because you're going to get dizzy." The boy groped desperately for a branch. His father supported him from beneath, and waited. The boy clambered. His feet scraped at the trunk. Then he was in the tree. Bark flakes and resin were stuck to the raw naked meat of his right hand. His father said:

"Now here, take this. Hurry."

The boy never knew whether his father himself had been frightened enough to forget for that moment about the boy's hand, or whether his father was still thinking quite clearly. His father may have expected that much. By the merciless clarity of his own standards, he may have expected that the boy should be able to hold onto a tree, and a wound, and a rifle, all with one hand. He extended the stock of the Winchester toward the boy.

The boy wanted to say something, but his tears and his fright would not let him gather a breath. He shuddered, and could not speak. "David," his father urged. The boy reached for the stock and faltered and clutched at the trunk with his good arm. He was crying and gasping, and he wanted to speak. He was afraid he would fall out of the tree. He released his grip once again, and felt himself tip. His father extended the gun higher, holding the barrel. The boy swung out his injured hand, spraying his father's face with blood. He reached and he tried to close torn dangling fingers around the stock and he pulled the trigger.

The bullet entered low on his father's thigh and shattered the knee and traveled down the shin bone and into the ground through his father's heel.

His father fell, and the rifle fell with him. He lay in the

snow without moving. The boy thought he was dead. Then the boy saw him grope for the rifle. He found it and rolled onto his stomach, taking aim at the sow grizzly. Forty feet up the hill, towering on hind legs, she canted her head to one side, indecisive. When the cub pulled itself up a snow-bank from the stream, she coughed at it sternly. The cub trotted straight to her with its head low. She knocked it off its feet with a huge paw, and it yelped. Then she turned quickly. The cub followed.

The woods were silent. The gunshot still echoed awesomely back to the boy but it was an echo of memory, not sound. He felt nothing. He saw his father's body stretched on the snow and he did not really believe he was where he was. He did not want to move: he wanted to wake. He sat in the tree and waited. The snow fell as gracefully as before.

His father rolled onto his back. The boy saw him raise himself to a sitting position and look down at the leg and betray no expression, and then slump back. He blinked slowly and lifted his eyes to meet the boy's eyes. The boy waited. He expected his father to speak. He expected his father to say *Shinny down using your elbows and knees and get the first-aid kit and hot water and phone the doctor. The number is taped to the dial.* His father stared. The boy could see the flicker of thoughts behind his father's eyes. His father said nothing. He raised his arms slowly and crossed them over his face, as though to nap in the sun.

The boy jumped. He landed hard on his feet and fell onto his back. He stood over his father. His hand dripped quietly onto the snow. He was afraid that his father was deciding to die. He wanted to beg him to reconsider. The boy had never before seen his father hopeless. He was afraid.

But he was no longer afraid of his father.

Then his father uncovered his face and said, "Let me see it."

They bandaged the boy's hand with a sleeve cut from the other arm of his shirt. His father wrapped the hand firmly and split the sleeve end with his deer knife and tied it neatly in two places. The boy now felt searing pain in his torn palm, and his stomach lifted when he thought of the damage, but at least he did not have to look at it. Quickly the plaid flannel bandage began to soak through maroon. They cut a sleeve from his father's shirt to tie over the wound in his thigh. They raised the trouser leg to see the long swelling bruise down the calf where he was hemorrhaging into the bullet's tunnel. Only then did his father realize that he was bleeding also from the heel. The boy took off his father's boot and placed a half-clean handkerchief on the insole where the bullet had exited, as his father instructed him. Then his father laced the boot on again tightly. The boy helped his father to stand. His father tried a step, then collapsed in the snow with a blasphemous howl of pain. They had not known that the knee was shattered.

The boy watched his father's chest heave with the forced sighs of suffocating frustration, and heard the air wheeze through his nostrils. His father relaxed himself with the breathing, and seemed to be thinking. He said,

"You can find your way back to the hut."

The boy held his own breath and did not move.

"You can, can't you?"

"But I'm not. I'm not going alone. I'm only going with you."

"All right, David, listen carefully," his father said. "We don't have to worry about freezing. I'm not worried about either of us freezing to death. No one is going to freeze in the woods in November, if he looks after himself. Not even in Montana. It just isn't that cold. I have matches and I have a fresh elk. And I don't think this weather is going to get any worse. It may be raining again by morning. What I'm concerned about is the bleeding. If I spend too much time and effort trying to walk out of here, I could bleed to death.

"I think your hand is going to be all right. It's a bad wound but the doctors will be able to fix it as good as new. I can see that. I promise you that. You'll be bleeding some too, but if you take care of that hand, it won't bleed any more walking than if you were standing still. Then you'll be at the doctor's tonight. But if I try to walk out on this leg it's going to bleed and keep bleeding and I'll lose too much blood. So I'm staying here and bundling up warm and you're walking out to get help. I'm sorry about this. It's what we have to do.

"You can't possibly get lost. You'll just follow this trail straight down the canyon the way we came up, and then you'll come to the meadow. Point yourself toward the big pine tree with the forked crown. When you get to that tree you'll find the creek again. You may not be able to see it, but make yourself quiet and listen for it. You'll hear it. Follow that down off the mountain and past the hut till you get to the jeep."

He struggled a hand into his pocket. "You've never driven a car, have you?"

The boy's lips were pinched. Muscles in his cheeks ached from clenching his jaws. He shook his head.

"You can do it. It isn't difficult." His father held up a single key and began telling the boy how to start the jeep, how to work the clutch, how to find reverse and then first and then second. As his father described the positions on the floor shift the boy raised his swaddled right hand. His father stopped. He rubbed at his eye sockets, like a man waking.

"Of course," he said. "All right. You'll have to help me."

Using the saw with his left hand, the boy cut a small forked aspen. His father showed the boy where to trim it so that the fork would reach just to his armpit. Then they lifted him to his feet. But the crutch was useless on a steep hillside of deep grass and snow. His father leaned over the boy's shoulders and they fought the slope for an hour.

When the boy stepped in a hole and they fell, his father made no exclamation of pain. The boy wondered whether his father's knee hurt as badly as his own hand. He suspected it hurt worse. He said nothing about his hand, though several times in their climb it was twisted or crushed. They reached the trail. The snow had not stopped, and their tracks were veiled. His father said:

"We need one of the guns. I forgot. It's my fault. But you'll have to go back down and get it."

The boy could not find the tree against which his father said he had leaned the .270, so he went toward the stream and looked for blood. He saw none. The imprint of his father's body was already softened beneath an inch of fresh silence. He scooped his good hand through the snowy depression and was startled by cool slimy blood, smearing his fingers like phlegm. Nearby he found the Winchester.

"The lucky one," his father said. "That's all right. Here." He snapped open the breech and a shell flew and he caught it in the air. He glanced dourly at the casing, then cast it aside in the snow. He held the gun out for the boy to see, and with his thumb let the hammer down one notch.

"Remember?" he said. "The safety."

The boy knew he was supposed to feel great shame, but he felt little. His father could no longer hurt him as he once could, because the boy was coming to understand him. His father could not help himself. He did not want the boy to feel contemptible, but he needed him to, because of the loneliness and the bitterness and the boy's mother; and he could not help himself.

After another hour they had barely traversed the aspen

hillside. Pushing the crutch away in angry frustration, his father sat in the snow. The boy did not know whether he was thinking carefully of how they might get him out, or still laboring with the choice against despair. The light had wilted to something more like moonlight than afternoon. The sweep of snow had gone gray, depthless, flat, and the sky warned sullenly of night. The boy grew restless. Then it was decided. His father hung himself piggyback over the boy's shoulders, holding the rifle. The boy supported him with elbows crooked under his father's knees. The boy was tall for eleven years old, and heavy. The boy's father weighed 164 pounds.

The boy walked.

He moved as slowly as drifting snow: a step, then time, then another step. The burden at first seemed to him overwhelming. He did not think he would be able to carry his father far.

He took the first few paces expecting to fall. He did not fall, so he kept walking. His arms and shoulders were not exhausted as quickly as he thought they would be, so he kept walking. Shuffling ahead in the deep powder was like carrying one end of an oak bureau up stairs. But for a surprisingly long time the burden did not grow any worse. He found balance. He found rhythm. He was moving.

Dark blurred the woods, but the snow was luminous. He could see the trail well. He walked.

"How are you, David? How are you holding up?"

"All right."

"We'll stop for a while and let you rest. You can set me down here." The boy kept walking. He moved so ponderously, it seemed after each step that he had stopped. But he kept walking.

"You can set me down. Don't you want to rest?"

The boy did not answer. He wished that his father would not make him talk. At the start he had gulped for air. Now he was breathing low and regularly. He was watching his thighs slice through the snow. He did not want to be disturbed. After a moment he said, "No."

He walked. He came to the dead cub, shrouded beneath new snow, and did not see it, and fell over it. His face was smashed deep into the snow by his father's weight. He could not move.

But he could breathe. He rested. When he felt his father's thigh roll across his right hand, he remembered the wound. He was lucky his arms had been pinned to his sides, or the hand might have taken the force of their fall. As he waited for his father to roll himself clear, the boy noticed the change in temperature. His sweat chilled him quickly. He began shivering.

His father had again fallen in silence. The boy knew that his father would not call out or even mention the pain in his leg. The boy realized that he did not want to mention his hand. The blood soaking the outside of his flannel bandage had grown sticky. He did not want to think of the alien tangle of flesh and tendons and bones wrapped inside. There was pain, but he kept the pain at a distance. It was not *his* hand anymore. He was not counting on ever having it back. If he was resolved about that, then the pain was not his either. It was merely pain of which he was aware. His good hand was numb.

"We'll rest now."

"I'm not tired," the boy said. "I'm just getting cold."

"We'll rest," said his father. "I'm tired."

Under his father's knee, the boy noticed, was a cavity in the snow, already melted away by fresh blood. The dark flannel around his father's thigh did not appear sticky. It gleamed.

His father instructed the boy how to open the cub with the deer knife. His father stood on one leg against a deadfall, holding the Winchester ready, and glanced around on all sides as he spoke. The boy used his left hand and both his knees. He punctured the cub low in the belly, to a soft squirting sound, and sliced upward easily. He did not gut the cub. He merely cut out a large square of belly meat. He handed it to his father, in exchange for the rifle.

His father peeled off the hide and left the fat. He sawed the meat in half. One piece he rolled up and put in his jacket pocket. The other he divided again. He gave the boy a square thick with glistening raw fat.

"Eat it. The fat too. Especially the fat. We'll cook the rest farther on. I don't want to build a fire here and taunt Momma."

The meat was chewy. The boy did not find it disgusting. He was hungry.

His father sat back on the ground and unlaced the boot from his good foot. Before the boy understood what he was doing, he had relaced the boot. He was holding a damp wool sock.

"Give me your left hand." The boy held out his good hand, and his father pulled the sock down over it. "It's getting a lot colder. And we need that hand."

"What about yours? We need your hands too. I'll give you my —"

"No, you won't. We need your feet more than anything. It's all right. I'll put mine inside your shirt."

He lifted his father, and they went on. The boy walked.

He moved steadily through cold darkness. Soon he was sweating again, down his ribs and inside his boots. Only his hands and ears felt as though crushed in a cold metal vise. But his father was shuddering. The boy stopped.

His father did not put down his legs. The boy stood on the trail and waited. Slowly he released his wrist holds. His father's thighs slumped. The boy was careful about the wounded leg. His father's grip over the boy's neck did not loosen. His fingers were cold against the boy's bare skin.

"Are we at the hut?"

"No. We're not even to the meadow."

"Why did you stop?" his father asked.

"It's so cold. You're shivering. Can we build a fire?"

"Yes," his father said hazily. "We'll rest. What time is it?"

"We don't know," the boy said. "We don't have a watch."

The boy gathered small deadwood. His father used the Winchester stock to scoop snow away from a boulder, and they placed the fire at the boulder's base. His father broke up pine twigs and fumbled dry toilet paper from his breast pocket and arranged the wood, but by then his fingers were shaking too badly to strike a match. The boy lit the fire. The boy stamped down the snow, as his father instructed, to make a small oven-like recess before the fire boulder. He cut fir boughs to floor the recess. He added more deadwood. Beyond the invisible clouds there seemed to be part of a moon.

"It stopped snowing," the boy said.

"Why?"

The boy did not speak. His father's voice had sounded unnatural. After a moment his father said:

"Yes, indeed. It stopped."

They roasted pieces of cub meat skewered on a green stick. Dripping fat made the fire spatter and flare. The meat was scorched on the outside and raw within. It tasted as good as any meat the boy had ever eaten. They burned their palates on hot fat. The second stick smoldered through before they had noticed, and that batch of meat fell in the fire. The boy's father cursed once and reached into the flame for it and dropped it and clawed it out, and then put his hand in the snow. He did not look at the blistered fingers. They ate. The boy saw that both his father's hands had gone clumsy and almost useless.

The boy went for more wood. He found a bleached deadfall not far off the trail, but with one arm he could only break up and carry small loads. They lay down in the recess together like spoons, the boy nearer the fire. They pulled fir boughs into place above them, resting across the snow. They pressed close together. The boy's father was shivering spastically now, and he clenched the boy in a fierce hug. The boy put his father's hands back inside his own shirt. The boy slept. He woke when the fire faded and added more wood and slept. He woke again and tended the fire and changed places with his father and slept. He slept less soundly with his father between him and the fire. He woke again when his father began to vomit.

The boy was terrified. His father wrenched with sudden vomiting that brought up cub meat and yellow liquid and blood and sprayed them across the snow by the grayish-red glow of the fire and emptied his stomach dry and then would not release him. He heaved on pathetically. The boy pleaded to be told what was wrong. His father could not or would not answer. The spasms seized him at the stomach and twisted the rest of his body taut in ugly jerks. Between the attacks he breathed with a wet rumbling sound deep in his chest, and did not speak. When the vomiting subsided, his breathing stretched itself out into long bubbling sighs, then shallow gasps, then more liquidy sighs. His breath caught and froth rose in his throat and into his mouth and he gagged on it and began vomiting again. The boy thought his father would choke. He knelt beside him and held him and cried. He could not see his father's face well and he did not want to look closely while the sounds that were coming from inside his father's body seemed so unhuman. The boy had never been more frightened. He wept for himself, and for his father. He knew from the noises and movements that his father must die. He did not think his father could ever be human again.

When his father was quiet, he went for more wood. He broke limbs from the deadfall with fanatic persistence and brought them back in bundles and built the fire up bigger. He nestled his father close to it and held him from behind. He did not sleep, though he was not awake. He waited. Finally he opened his eyes on the beginnings of dawn. His father sat up and began to spit.

"One more load of wood and you keep me warm from behind and then we'll go."

The boy obeyed. He was surprised that his father could speak. He thought it strange now that his father was so concerned for himself and so little concerned for the boy. His father had not even asked how he was.

The boy lifted his father, and walked.

Sometime while dawn was completing itself, the snow had resumed. It did not filter down soundlessly. It came on a slight wind at the boy's back, blowing down the canyon. He felt as though he were tumbling forward with the snow into a long vertical shaft. He tumbled slowly. His father's body protected the boy's back from being chilled by the wind. They were both soaked through their clothes. His father was soon shuddering again.

The boy walked. Muscles down the back of his neck were sore from yesterday. His arms ached, and his shoulders and thighs, but his neck hurt him most. He bent his head forward against the weight and the pain, and he watched his legs surge through the snow. At his stomach he felt the dull ache of hunger, not as an appetite but as an affliction. He thought of the jeep. He walked.

He recognized the edge of the meadow but through the snow-laden wind he could not see the cluster of aspens. The snow became deeper where he left the wooded trail. The direction of the wind was now variable, sometimes driving snow into his face, sometimes whipping across him from the right. The grass and snow dragged at his thighs, and he moved by stumbling forward and then catching himself back. Twice he stepped into small overhung fingerlets of the stream, and fell violently, shocking the air from his lungs and once nearly spraining an ankle. Farther out into the meadow, he saw the aspens. They were a hundred yards off to his right. He did not turn directly toward them. He was afraid of crossing more hidden creeks on the intervening ground. He was not certain now whether the main channel was between him and the aspen grove or behind him to the left. He tried to project from the canyon trail to the aspens and on to the forked pine on the far side of the meadow, along what he remembered as almost a straight line. He pointed himself toward the far edge, where the pine should have been. He could not see a forked crown. He could not even see trees. He could see only a vague darker corona above the curve of white. He walked.

He passed the aspens and left them behind. He stopped several times with the wind rasping against him in the open meadow, and rested. He did not set his father down. His father was trembling uncontrollably. He had not spoken for a long time. The boy wanted badly to reach the far side of the meadow. His socks were soaked and his boots and cuffs were glazed with ice. The wind was chafing his face and making him dizzy. His thighs felt as if they had been bruised with a club. The boy wanted to give up and set his father down and whimper that this had gotten to be very unfair; and he wanted to reach the far trees. He did not doubt which he would do. He walked.

He saw trees. Raising his head painfully, he squinted against the rushing flakes. He did not see the forked crown.

He went on, and stopped again, and craned his neck, and squinted. He scanned a wide angle of pines, back and forth. He did not see it. He turned his body and his burden to look back. The snow blew across the meadow and seemed, whichever way he turned, to be streaking into his face. He pinched his eyes tighter. He could still see the aspens. But he could not judge where the canyon trail met the meadow. He did not know from just where he had come. He looked again at the aspens, and then ahead to the pines. He considered the problem carefully. He was irritated that the forked ponderosa did not show itself yet, but not worried. He was forced to estimate. He estimated, and went on in that direction.

When he saw a forked pine it was far off to the left of his course. He turned and marched toward it gratefully. As he came nearer, he bent his head up to look. He stopped. The boy was not sure that this was the right tree. Nothing about it looked different, except the thick cakes of snow weighting its limbs, and nothing about it looked especially familiar. He had seen thousands of pine trees in the last few days. This was one like the others. It definitely had a forked crown. He entered the woods at its base.

He had vaguely expected to join a trail. There was no trail. After two hundred yards he was still picking his way among trees and deadfalls and brush. He remembered the shepherd's creek that fell off the lip of the meadow and led down the first canyon. He turned and retraced his tracks to the forked pine.

He looked for the creek. He did not see it anywhere near the tree. He made himself quiet, and listened. He heard nothing but wind, and his father's tremulous breathing.

"Where is the creek?"

His father did not respond. The boy bounced gently up and down, hoping to jar him alert.

"Where is the creek? I can't find it."

"What?"

"We crossed the meadow and I found the tree but I can't find the creek. I need you to help."

"The compass is in my pocket," his father said.

He lowered his father into the snow. He found the compass in his father's breast pocket, and opened the flap, and held it level. The boy noticed with a flinch that his right thigh was smeared with fresh blood. For an instant he thought he had a new wound. Then he realized that the blood was his father's. The compass needle quieted.

"What do I do?"

His father did not respond. The boy asked again. His father said nothing. He sat in the snow and shivered.

The boy left his father and made random arcs within sight of the forked tree until he found a creek. They followed it onward along the flat and then where it gradually began sloping away. The boy did not see what else he could do. He knew that this was the wrong creek. He hoped that it would flow into the shepherd's creek, or at least bring them out on the same road where they had left the jeep. He was very tired. He did not want to stop. He did not care any more about being warm. He wanted only to reach the jeep, and to save his father's life.

He wondered whether his father would love him more generously for having done it. He wondered whether his father would ever forgive him for having done it.

If he failed, his father could never again make him feel shame, the boy thought naively. So he did not worry about failing. He did not worry about dying. His hand was not bleeding, and he felt strong. The creek swung off and down to the left. He followed it, knowing that he was lost. He did not want to reverse himself. He knew that turning back would make him feel confused and desperate and frightened.

As long as he was following some pathway, walking, going down, he felt strong.

That afternoon he killed a grouse. He knocked it off a low branch with a heavy short stick that he threw like a boomerang. The grouse fell in the snow and floundered and the boy ran up and plunged on it. He felt it thrashing against his chest. He reached in and it nipped him and he caught it by the neck and squeezed and wrenched mercilessly until long after it stopped writhing. He cleaned it as he had seen his father clean grouse and built a small fire with matches from his father's breast pocket and seared the grouse on a stick. He fed his father. His father could not chew. The boy chewed mouthfuls of grouse, and took the chewed gobbets in his hand, and put them into his father's mouth. His father could swallow. His father could no longer speak.

The boy walked. He thought of his mother in Evergreen Park, and at once he felt queasy and weak. He thought of his mother's face and her voice as she was told that her son was lost in the woods in Montana with a damaged hand that would never be right, and with his father, who had been shot and was unconscious and dying. He pictured his mother receiving the news that her son might die himself, unless he could carry his father out of the woods and find his way to the jeep. He saw her face change. He heard her voice. The boy had to stop. He was crying. He could not control the shape of his mouth. He was not crying with true sorrow, as he had in the night when he held his father and thought his father would die; he was crying in sentimental self-pity. He sensed the difference. Still he cried.

He must not think of his mother, the boy realized. Thinking of her could only weaken him. If she knew where he was, what he had to do, she could only make it impossible for him to do it. He was lucky that she knew nothing, the boy thought.

No one knew what the boy was doing, or what he had yet to do. Even the boy's father no longer knew. The boy was lucky. No one was watching, no one knew, and he was free to be capable.

The boy imagined himself alone at his father's grave. The grave was open. His father's casket had already been lowered. The boy stood at the foot in his black Christmas suit, and his hands were crossed at his groin, and he was not crying. Men with shovels stood back from the grave, waiting for the boy's order for them to begin filling it. The boy felt a horrible swelling sense of joy. The men watched him, and he stared down into the hole. He knew it was a lie. If his father died, the boy's mother would rush out to Livingston and have him buried and stand at the grave in a black dress and veil squeezing the boy to her side like he was a child. There was nothing the boy could do about that. All the more reason he must keep walking.

Then she would tow the boy back with her to Evergreen Park. And he would be standing on 96th Street in the morning dark before his father's cold body had even begun to grow alien and decayed in the buried box. She would drag him back, and there would be nothing the boy could do. And he realized that if he returned with his mother after the burial, he would never again see the cabin outside Livingston. He would have no more summers and no more Novembers anywhere but in Evergreen Park.

The cabin now seemed to be at the center of the boy's life. It seemed to stand halfway between this snowbound creek valley and the train station in Chicago. It would be his cabin soon.

The boy knew nothing about his father's will, and he had never been told that legal ownership of the cabin was destined for him. Legal ownership did not matter. The cabin might be owned by his mother, or sold to pay his father's debts, or taken away by the state, but it would still be the boy's cabin. It could only forever belong to him. His father had been telling him *Here, this is yours. Prepare to receive it.* The boy had sensed that much. But he had been threatened, and unwilling. The boy realized now that he might be resting warm in the cabin in a matter of hours, or he might never see it again. He could appreciate the justice of that. He walked.

He thought of his father as though his father were far away from him. He saw himself in the black suit at the grave, and he heard his father speak to him from aside: *That's good. Now raise your eyes and tell them in a man's voice to begin shoveling. Then turn away and walk slowly back down the hill. Be sure you don't cry. That's good.* The boy stopped. He felt his glands quiver, full of new tears. He knew that it was a lie. His father would never be there to congratulate him. His father would never know how well the boy had done.

He took deep breaths. He settled himself. Yes, his father would know somehow, the boy believed. His father had known all along. His father knew.

He built the recess just as they had the night before, except this time he found flat space between a stone bank and a large fallen cottonwood trunk. He scooped out the snow, he laid boughs, and he made a fire against each reflector. At first the bed was quite warm. Then the melt from the fires began to run down and collect in the middle, forming a puddle of wet boughs under them. The boy got up and carved runnels across the packed snow to drain the fires. He went back to sleep and slept warm, holding his father. He rose again each half hour to feed the fires.

The snow stopped in the night, and did not resume. The woods seemed to grow quieter, settling, sighing beneath the new weight. What was going to come had come.

The boy grew tired of breaking deadwood and began walking again before dawn and walked for five more hours. He did not try to kill the grouse that he saw because he did not want to spend time cleaning and cooking it. He was hurrying now. He drank from the creek. At one point he found small black insects like winged ants crawling in great numbers across the snow near the creek. He stopped to pinch up and eat thirty or forty of them. They were tasteless. He did not bother to feed any to his father. He felt he had come a long way down the mountain. He thought he was reaching the level now where there might be roads. He followed the creek, which had received other branches and grown to a stream. The ground was flattening again and the drainage was widening, opening to daylight. As he carried his father, his head ached. He had stopped noticing most of his other pains. About noon of that day he came to the fence.

It startled him. He glanced around, his pulse drumming suddenly, preparing himself at once to see the long empty sweep of snow and broken fence posts and thinking of Basque shepherds fifty years gone. He saw the cabin and the smoke. He relaxed, trembling helplessly into laughter. He relaxed, and was unable to move. Then he cried, still laughing. He cried shamelessly with relief and dull joy and wonder, for as long as he wanted. He held his father, and cried. But he set his father down and washed his own face with snow before he went to the door.

He crossed the lot walking slowly, carrying his father. He did not now feel tired.

The young woman's face was drawn down in shock and revealed at first nothing of friendliness.

"We had a jeep parked somewhere, but I can't find it," the boy said. "This is my father."

THEY WOULD NOT TALK to him. They stripped him and put him before the fire wrapped in blankets and started tea and made him wait. He wanted to talk. He wished they would ask him a lot of questions. But they went about quickly and quietly, making things warm. His father was in the bedroom.

The man with the face full of dark beard had used the radio to call for a doctor. He went back into the bedroom with more blankets, and stayed. His wife went from room to room with hot tea. She rubbed the boy's naked shoulders through the blanket, and held a cup to his mouth, but she would not talk to him. He did not know what to say to her, and he could not move his lips very well. But he wished she would ask him some questions. He was restless, thawing in silence before the hearth.

He thought about going back to their own cabin soon. In his mind he gave the bearded man directions to take him and his father home. It wasn't far. It would not require much of the man's time. They would thank him, and give him an elk steak. Later he and his father would come back for the jeep. He could keep his father warm at the cabin as well as they were doing here, the boy knew.

While the woman was in the bedroom, the boy overheard the bearded man raise his voice:

"He what?"

"He carried him out," the woman whispered.

"What do you mean, carried him?"

"Carried him. On his back. I saw."

"Carried him from where?"

"Where it happened. Somewhere on Sheep Creek, maybe."

"Eight miles?"

"I know."

"*Eight miles*? How could he do that?"

"I don't know. I suppose he couldn't. But he did."

The doctor arrived in half an hour, as the boy was just starting to shiver. The doctor went into the bedroom and stayed five minutes. The woman poured the boy more tea and knelt beside him and hugged him around the shoulders.

When the doctor came out, he examined the boy without speaking. The boy wished the doctor would ask him some questions, but he was afraid he might be shivering too hard to answer in a man's voice. While the doctor touched him and probed him and took his temperature, the boy looked the doctor directly in the eye, as though to show him he was really all right.

The doctor said:

"David, your father is dead. He has been dead for a long time. Probably since yesterday."

"I know that," the boy said.

✍ Nathan's Rime ✍

LIKE A SHREW EATS, Nathan talked: as though, because of the character of his metabolism, if he stopped for a few hours, he would die. His manic chatter attached like a lien, evidently, on the title to this patch of mountainside. It wasn't what the new owner had bargained for.

Buddy Coop was buying this land with the last of his father's estate, a modest bit of money that until very recently had sat ignored, in a Denver bank, for nine years. He had put it there himself after liquidating, in a moment of sorrowed petulance, the last physical token of a Coop family past. His final act before leaving the state. Then nine years of interest, nine years of inflation, nine years of regret had factored themselves upon that middling principal: proceeds from the sale of the cabin in which his father had killed himself. In today's dollars it bought ninety acres of scrawny Oregon lodgepole, a stagnant bog which had once been a pond, a hermit's shack. And, apparently, Nathan. But one emotional lien, the one still held by his father, was already too many.

Days passed as Buddy tried to clamp his mind shut while continuing work. Nathan, old man in a filthy tweed jacket, weathered and angular as the shack, tortured him with talk.

The whole performance seemed impelled by some source of desperation, and foreshortened by some source of haste. None of it made a great deal of sense. An unidentified man figured centrally, a younger woman, railroad cars in the desert, a murder in California. By the end of their first long camp-fire evening Buddy understood only this: that Nathan's consciousness was inhabited, like the state of Texas, mainly by snakes.

NATHAN SAID:

"I run off to live amongst pigs. I was just eleven. Pigs, I mean, real swine. Slept overnight in the mud and the filth of the pen, with a sow and her litter. Sniffing me there in the dark, growling her pig noises. Ready to nip and snarl protecting the young. Fearsome creatures, big swine are, when you crowd them. Then I was drug out, at daylight, and brung on back. It was a neighbor woman's sow pen. I took a whipping. He whipped my tail pussing raw. Whipped me to bleed, with that old brass-head cane.

"I knew he would do her. But I feared them snakes so. I was big eyed and Christmas-skittish with fear. Could not hold my water at night in the bed. And eleven years old. I thought it was work of the Fiend he was at, keeping them serpents. Or I didn't know what."

Buddy stared into the embers. He was sitting on the ground, elbows hooked back over the log on which Nathan squatted. "I don't understand. If they were filthy and vicious, why did you hide in a pigpen?"

"Look at a pig," Nathan said.

"Sure. Not a comely animal. I agree. I would never bed down with one."

"Skin a pig out," Nathan said. "A pig is armored with fat. Layer of fat as thick as a sponge. No veins in it. A pig can

46

take rattler bites all day long. Just so it ain't on the tip of the snout. Don't even make her sick. A pig is a natural snake killer. Snarf rattlers like link sausage, quick as lunch, and not give it a thought. Well, a rattler knows that. You don't see him go near a pig. Not even in Texas, ankle-deep with snakes everywhere, you don't see it. A animal knows its enemies. And a rattlesnake knows a pig."

Nathan poked at the coals with his boot. Small flecks of orange fire floated up the invisible fountain of heat, through the darkness, disappearing above in the sky-black gap between branches. He pushed the charred nub of a log into the circle. He seemed to be tracing back across thoughts from which Buddy's question had diverted him.

"That old brass-head cane," he repeated. "Merciful God." For a moment an old man gaped at his memories.

"When I come ten years of age, he said I was big enough to squirt down the pit." New flames arose, reflected in the brushfire brown of Nathan's eyes. "Till then, my chores was just to look after the racers and rat snakes and hog-nosers. He kept me away from the rattlers and copperheads and all, 'cause he said I didn't know what I was doing. And he was right. I cleaned out the cages after them gentle snakes, fed them, fed the tarantulas and the scorpion too, and that didn't bother me so bad. Then he come and say I was ready to squirt down the pit.

"That must of been two or three years. He took me down there to Bromfuss when I would just of been going to school. He told my momma he won the place in a card game, from a man who hated the Mexicans and so he wanted to leave and go off to Joplin or somewhere. The whole place, the sleeper cars and the cages and the turnstile and the peanut machine and four dozen hungry snakes, they was all in the pot of this poker game, he told her. But I knew that for a lie, later on.

Because a man come round every month, when we first was there, to take money off him for the place. And that man did for a fact hate the Mexicans.

"He and my momma had such a row, and we left. We hitch-hiked ourselves down there to Bromfuss, and ate Nab crackers and jerky till the first customer come. There was two sleeper cars from the Gulf and Chicago Railroad, and one of them had its walls chopped out on the inside, and chicken wire cages built out of vegetable crates stuck up on these plank shelves that run all the length on both sides. Just like a railroad museum car for the Southern Line that I seen once in Austin. Only instead of them little toy engines and old pictures and cuspidors and a gold spike that was driven to connect up the lines at Amarillo, there was snakes, if you can imagine. Hunger-starved snakes all over the floor, and sashaying around loose, when we got there, and a six-foot diamondback met us at the door. It looked like that man with the Mexicans must of gone out of the snake business all of a sudden.

"He got us some customers in there, but not many. We took a dime a head off them, a nickel for kids that could walk under the turnstile, and they could look for as long as they wanted. Some spent as much as a hour, drifting up and down in front of them cages, asking a question about this snake or that other, like they was trying to use up two bits worth of snake-watching for their dime. But he figured, Let them stay, if they sleep here tonight they'll have to buy peanuts for supper. The peanuts was a nickel, and cold drinks was another dime. The gorilla dolls and rhinoceros coin banks was a quarter. So he didn't care if they stayed a week.

"Pretty soon he bought a old barn. We tore it down, and dragged the lumber up there, and got it rebuilt as sort of a long skinny shed, twice as big as the sleeper car. We moved the snakes into that shed, and he built some more chickenwire cages. Because he was learning to catch him his own snakes, merciful God help me. He had got into the snake business with both of his boots.

"He chopped out the back of the old sleeper and put up a corral for the buffalo and the longhorn. Because a man had come through in a truck, who said he could give him a bargain deal on a buffalo. And some folks, the man said, don't like to come and just look at lizards and spiders and scorpions. They want to see a animal with some hair. And he said, A tarantula has all the hair you could want. And besides, I got a bear in a concrete pen, right out back. But some folks, the man said, like to see a friendly animal or two, a household-type animal, along with their lizards and bears. So he bought the buffalo and the longhorn. All the first-class snake farms in Texas and Arizona, the man said, and he said he had visited most of them himself, they all have a buffalo. And in Louisiana they have alligators. His eyes went big as fried eggs when he heard that, and he asked if the man had him a bargain alligator to sell. But the man didn't, praise God.

"And when the shed was full of them new cages, he got him a gallon of parakeet-green paint and climbed up on the front, and I held the ladder for a whole day of work while he painted the words BUCKLES WORLDWIDE SERPENTARIUM in smart letters. And then he walked to the other side of the highway and admired his sign, till it got dark.

"Not long after that a man with a Arkansas accent come in and said, 'Are you Mr. Buckles?' And he said, 'No.' He said, 'My name is Buckle.' And the man asked him what to God was a serpentarium. This fellow was a city man from Little Rock, it turned out. 'That's where a snake lives,' he said. 'Oh,' the man said. 'I thought that was a old barn.' And the man laughed. 'It use to be,' he said. 'Now it's a serpentarium.' After that the man wanted to know what was so worldwide about it. And he said that would cost him a dime to find out. The Arkansas man didn't laugh then. He stalled around the turnstile for a bit with his hands in his pockets, and he went back outside once to stare up at the sign. But finally that man give him the dime. He took the Arkansas man down the row and pointed to a cage. 'You see that black-tail rattlesnake there,' he said. The man bent over and squinted through the chickenwire. Then the man said yep, he saw the rattler. 'Well, they got black-tail rattlers just like that one there in the country of Mexico,' he said.

"And the next day he got back up the ladder to paint the picture of a snake right under his sign. Because he was worried about other city folks not knowing right off what a serpentarium was, he said. He painted a parakeet-green cobra. He copied the picture out of this book he had got from San Antone, with the cobra up on its neck to strike at you and its head spread out flat like a wood spoon. When he come down off the ladder I said, 'But we ain't got no cobra. Alls we got are these rattlers and king snakes and copperheads. How come you made a cobra if we don't even got one?' And he said, 'Well we got one now.'

"He commenced to take in some money. People going by on the highway between Austin and San Antone begun to stop for a look at the serpentarium. They paid their dime, and they bought their peanuts. We had a salesman stopped twice a week, just for a cold drink. But he drunk that standing outside the turnstile. And then there was this carload of folks in tuxedos, and the women in shiny dresses, that stopped in one night like it was a house party, and all paid their dimes to get in. They walked up and down and gawked at the cages, laughing among themselves, and the women made female noises at sight of the snakes, and they bought cold drinks as set-ups for what they had brung along with them. These folks stayed for maybe a half hour, drinking and laughing and strolling around like it was New Year's at a hotel. Then they thanked him kindly, and left. But on the way out, they saw me, holding a pail of water, so one of them give me a tip. A woman in a silver dress, she give me a dime tip for carrying water at a serpentarium. And that beat all.

"We closed up about dark, and he went out himself, most every night except when the moon was full, with a gunny sack. He would come back after daylight with more snakes. He did that till the cages was all full. And he never yet had got bit. He found his way about in the snake business real quick, it seemed. He was naturally good at snakes. He could tell three kinds of king snake and about three kinds of rattler and two kinds of copperhead, and just which one would kill a man how fast. And I'll tell you what else. He got so he could tell him a man snake from a female. And I still to this day don't know how he done that.

"He had got to be just a snaking fool. Then he went into Bromfuss one day, and the next thing I knew he had that old brass-head cane, from a junk store. Carried it about like a riverboat dandy. It was hard knobbled hickory, and it stung like the wrath of God. It had the head of a rattlesnake, cast out of pure brass, for a handle. That's why he bought it. He carried it like he was Sam Houston, with that brass rattler heavy and snug in his palm.

"But most all of the snakes he was catching was diamondbacks. He found that out from his book. First he said, Woo, I have me a collection of diamondback rattlesnakes. If diamondbacks are money, then I'm a rich man. But later he got to saying, Buffalo-dump, I am tired of these diamondbacks. And then he would mope in from a night of stumbling around in the bushes and gulleys, and his sack would go thump on the floor, and he only would say, Diamondbacks.

Yellow-belly king snakes, he found them when he didn't find diamondbacks, and sometimes he got him a racer. But mostly more diamondbacks. We was eating diamondbacks for supper, skinned out and fried in lard, and all the cages was full, and still more diamondbacks. He had this book showed pictures of every snake between the Panama Canal and the Canada border, and he coveted them every one, and here he was up to his knuckles in diamondbacks. Texas has all the world's diamondbacks, I think, and we must of et up a good part of them that year. He was going to have to change the picture out front, pretty soon, and maybe the name of the place, to BUCKLES DIAMONDBACK KENNELS. So he got him the idea for the pit.

"He paid a man to pour it in concrete right off the back door of the shed. It was dug into the ground six feet deep, and it had a wall all around it four feet high. Texas don't make the snake that can climb ten feet of concrete. In the center there was a sewer drain, so the snakes wouldn't drown in the winter. But he hadn't yet told me what he was thinking of. I said, you ain't fixing to go off to Louisiana and bring back a alligator, are you? He said no. I said, Is that for us? Is that a swimming-bath? And he laughed and said no. He said I would see whose swimming-bath it would be. Then when the concrete dried, he took all his diamondbacks out of the cages, and all his king snakes, and chucked them down there in the bottom. So we didn't have to eat snake-flesh no more. And he called it the pit.

"He set up a vegetable scale with a round pan, hanging over that pit. And he let it get into Bromfuss that he would pay folks for their snakes. He would pay top price for snakes they brought him, and double top price for any brand of snake where he didn't already have one. But for their diamondbacks, he would pay three cents a pound.

"And still he never yet had got bit. Once every second Saturday he took a stepladder and climbed down into his pit with a garden hose, and squirted it off to the sewer drain, because of the filth and the smell. All those diamondbacks right there with him, thick as manure on a barn floor, and he would shuffle around and ease them from underfoot with his brass-head cane, and watch where he stepped, and then he would squirt them snakes in the eye with cold water till their mottle showed up again and they went mad as bees. And he'd laugh. That was his fun. But he saw to it people rode out there on Saturday and watched him climb down into the pit. And they paid a dime each for the privilege.

"So finally he got bit. He had come to be too confident, and he forgot that the tooth of one snake can kill a man, whether he worries or no. He was in the pit. He had the cane in his hand and I was waiting to give him the garden hose, but he wasn't done moving the snakes around, pulling them off the wall where they tried to scooch up, and stacking them over to one side like old bicycle tubes. He was using his bare hand, 'cause nine people had come out to watch. He would tap a snake on the back of the head, real quick and smart with his bare hand, and that snake would fall down off the wall. Using his bare hand that way, when he had the cane, them nine people just thought he was Mister Magic. And then he played it on one snake too many. This snake was six and a half feet long, and it was ornery. It caught him flat in the palm. Nine people saw how.

"And later he called it his ninety-cent bite. He claimed he wouldn't be bit again for less than three dollars. That was after his arm finished swelling up to the shoulder, and most of his hand turned the color and smell of dead rabbit. It was later he told the jokes. Meantime his thumb very near to rotted right off the hand.

"We thought it was gone. That snake had got a fang in

there, and the fleshy part that connected it up to the rest of the hand went to rot like a piece of fruit, streaming and sweating and smelling and shrinking back off the bone. You could see his thumb bone right there inside, plain as anything, for up to a week. If the bone started to rot too, he said, the thumb is a goner, so I'll go into town and have a doctor chop off the hand. He watched it for another two weeks, reading in his books about snakebite and leaving me with the heavy chores. But the bone never went to rot. It seem to come near. That thumb dangled loose for a good while with less than half its flesh. But it stayed on the hand. Then it begun to grow back.

"And the whole time he raved in his fever, five or six days after he got bit, he would not let me close up the snake farm for business, nor send into Bromfuss for the doctor. Because he said it would hurt the trade, word getting out and around that the serpentaryist was dying of snakebite. So I sat over there on a stool by the turnstile, and took the dimes and sold the cold drinks, and when folks asked where he was I said he was busy out back, and meantime he lay on his bed in the Gulf and Chicago sleeper car and swoll up and fevered and foamed and raved. And when the fever passed off for a while and I brought him some bean soup, he would say, Are we open for business? And I'd say, Yeah we are. And he would say, That's right. And I thought, But what if you die? I ain't going to sit on that stool and take no more dimes if you die, and I don't care what. And I thought, But what else will I do?

"He never did take a remedy for that snakebite. He never let me go for the doctor and he never put nothing on it and he never et nothing that whole week but bean soup and saltines and hard-boil eggs and coffee. And he did not take a swallow of whiskey. Then he was better. His thumb grew back just like before.

"That all must of been two or three years. When I come ten, he saw that I had got big, so he said, Nathan, I believe yer ready to squirt down the pit. Ain't you, boy? I didn't say nothing. I didn't fancy to climb down into no concrete hole full of serpents and get me a ninety-cent bite. Because I had seen him rave, and I had seen his flesh rot, and I had thought he would die. But he said I was going to do her. And he didn't have no people out there this time, at a dime each. He sent me down on a Monday. He even closed up the front door for business, and he brought the stepladder and set it down in there, and he put the garden hose in my hand, and he said, Just watch where you set yer feet. It was all right, he said. Because a snake is not like a mad dog or a man: a snake don't bite you except for a reason.

"He had sat me up on the edge of the wall. And below me was more diamondbacks than two men could eat in a year. And I said, It don't look all that dirty. It was dirty enough, he said. But not so dirty it would take me much time at all, once I got to it. I had one foot on the ladder and one hand wrapped on his wrist just as tight as a little monkey, and I was terrified like I don't know what, praying God he would not give me a shove. I didn't say nothing. He waited, and then he said, Nathan. Let's go, boy. You be fourteen, at this rate, by the time you get to the bottom. And I thought, Fourteen. I want to be fourteen. And still I didn't say nothing. He said again, Let's go, boy. And it was then I squeezed down on his wrist like a little chimpanzee, and I said, Give me the brass-head cane.

"But he would not. He would not. Because he said it was just his. He got me a broomstick from the yard, and he said, This here is just as good as any old brass-head cane. This here can be yer own snaking stick, Nathan. Now let's go, boy, he said.

"So I climbed down to squirt out the pit.

"And it was a year of that till I run off. I never yet had got bit. But I saw diamondbacks in my dreams, that would move at me, and I would snatch back, and knock myself wide awake. I soiled the bedclothes, and eleven years old. Every second Saturday I went down into that pit, and walked about on my tippy-toes and hardly drew breath for an hour. I wasn't like him. I didn't never come to be too confident. When I was in the pit on a day, that night I would cry like a baby. Because I was so glad at having got it over this time, and I was so dreading of having to go down there again the next second Saturday, that I didn't know what. One year of them second Saturdays, then I lit out.

"I went on a Friday night. But he let the pit go to filth till he had me back, and the welts from that brass-head cane had scabbed over, and I could put on a pair of trousers. I just had to squirt it on Tuesday."

AND NATHAN SAID:

"So after he got us the old Chevy taxicab we would go snaking all the way down there to Terrel County, just this side of the river from Mexico. I don't recall where he first heard about Terrel County. Some snakers from Oklahoma stopped in at Bromfuss on their way home, I expect, and they put the name into his ear. To get there you went down below San Antone and out through Del Rio and crossed the Pecos and stopped for more water and gas in a settlement town called Langtry, named after a music hall woman. You used up a day on the road and two spare tires getting you that far. Beyond Langtry was just desert and dry washes and a few dirt roads that led out to nowhere and back. And more snakes in them hills and gulches than God has fingers to count them on. And that's why he took us to Terrel County.

"We would close up the serpentarium and go off, snaking day and night for up to a week. I lived on Nehi and Vienna sausages out of these bitty cans, from the Langtry store, and he ate sardines packed with green chilies. He slept right there on the ground, wherever we stopped at the end of a night, but I slept in the taxicab, for fear of scorpions. Till the taxicab got filled up with snake bags and tarantula shoeboxes. And then I slept on the ground too.

"It was a old yellow '26 Chevy, with a black top and a white bubble and a kick seat that had got tore out in a scuffle, and lettered across the side BEATRICE CAB CO. DALLAS—FT. WORTH. He got it for sixty dollars. It had a sprung left forward spring, but it took them dirt and rock roads like a farm truck, that taxicab. Roads that sometimes you couldn't tell roadbed from dry wash. When we snaked, he would beat it along them roads for most of a night, me hanging out one window and him the other, looking to catch sight of a snake as it crossed over the road. Then maybe I holler out, or he catches sight of a dark skinny something, and screech goes his foot on the brake, into reverse, and he guns her straight back through the dust cloud. Out we pile with our sticks and sacks to take prisoners from amongst the surviving, if there are any. He flattened quite a number of snakes, backing up that way, and a tarantula that went off like a Silver Salute, before he ever got careful. He always was in a hurry.

"So he made him a fancy collection of Mexican snakes, roaring round them dark roads with a taxicab full of gunny sacks, and the serpentarium business was good. People come out from Bromfuss, come up from San Antone, some even come down from Austin, to see his Mexican snakes. He had a rabbit hutch full of tarantulas, thick as brown fur all over the bottom, and he sold them for pets at thirty cents each.

Yes, some folks did in fact want a tarantula for a pet. It beat me to know why. And he got him a scarlet thunder centipede, look like a coral snake with these hundred bitty legs, and a Mexican poison toad, look like a hop toad with the cholera. Truthfully, he had such a collection of outlandish vermin by now, it was enough to make a man sick. But he wasn't done.

"Then one night in Terrel County we had a good load, and the back of the taxi was heaped down with snakes, all heavy and cool and quiet like fresh cowpies steaming inside the cloth sacks. There was a Blair's king snake and a couple red racers and four big Mojave rattlers. He pulled off the road at a fording and drove on up the dry wash a ways, for us to bed down. We never had done a better night's snaking. We dropped off to sleep under our blankets, and the sand was a soft bed.

"I woke when I heard him bark 'Nathan!' and it was light. All I saw was the seat of his trousers, him already off at a gallop toward the taxicab. I thought it must be a cougar or somesuch that had made him lit out, and I snapped around. But there was nothing. I didn't know what. And then I felt it, underneath me. In the ground itself. I was up and got my legs moving just as that big ball of flood rounded the corner and bore down.

"It came on through the wash like the tongue of a giant longhorn, all red and dusty and fat, and singing a low awful grumble as it came. It moved fast as a freight train.

"I made the bank and I looked. But he had run straight down the wash, for the taxicab. He jumped in and closed the door tight. He went to work on the starter button. The flood came on like thunder. He spun the wheels in the sand, then the taxi was moving. I thought, My dear God, he won't give up them snakes to no flood if it takes his life. But the taxi was rolling, and he wound it up to about thirty-five miles per hour before he got to the road. The flood came ahead, it closed on him, but he beat it, almost. It caught him only a splash, that lifted the rear end. Right then he hit the ford, with his tail coming up on his left, and he sailed over the road like a stunt driver. I saw the two feet of water and daylight open up under his wheels. Then he was back on the ground again, straddling the far bank and fighting his rear end around neat as you please. He caught the bank and went on, and the flood gushed by just short of him, and he piled the taxicab slam into a big cottonwood.

"Broke his shoulder against the wheel. And them tarantula shoeboxes was up-ended all over everywhere, when I got to him. He had cracked that old taxicab's engine right off its mount. But down under the seat there, looped up heavy and cool, them snakes was good as new.

"Then we didn't go down to Terrel County no more. I was fourteen years old by now. I had made my peace with the rattlers in the pit. I did what he said, and I did not try to run off. I just treated them rattlers like poisonous snakes. But then this other thing.

"A crate come, from all the way over to Africa, and his arm still in a sling from that cottonwood, so he said, Nathan, you go open that, boy. Just you be careful.

"He had bought forty-five dollars of African snakemeat off a Portuguese man over there, and the box was nearly three months in the mail. The man packed his snakes in burlap coffee sacks, and they seem to got on without food nor water nor nothing. He already had got two other crates of good healthy snakemeat off the same man. This time it was African mambas, green ones and the black ones about even. But just for a extra the man packed in this other, or for a joke, or I never did know why. I went after the lid with a bar. I stood back. When I come round to peek in and saw a hump of dark there inside, my hand cocked back with the bar. But it wasn't no African mamba. It was something I never expected. It was just the carcass of that old two-headed monkey."

Buddy straightened his spine. Bright hot afternoon now, and he was at work, carving a stairway into the steep cliffside between his land and the fire road: cutting brush, moving dirt, staking split logs into place as steps. His hair was soaked with sweat and ten minutes earlier he had folded back his left thumbnail. He said:

"Nathan. In three seconds I open your skull with this shovel if you haven't retracted the monkey. There were snakes, okay, and madness in plenitude, yes. But there was no two-headed monkey.

"It was the carcass of a two-headed baby monkey." Nathan spoke to the cliffside with righteous certainty. "Before God. It was dried like a prune."

"Hand me that split. I don't believe a word of it, Nathan. I don't even hear you. Hand me that split, there."

Nathan made a perfunctory prod with his boot. The length of split pine slid six inches toward Buddy, then lazed over sideways and began tumbling down the slope. Buddy went onto a knee, reached, pinned the log for a second before its weight swung it around free, and on. It rolled. Nathan and he watched without further comment, five or six seconds, as the log bobbed away dreamily, speeding and leaping, falling to rest finally in the grassy flat at the base of the cliffside.

Buddy glowered downhill, then at Nathan. Who said:

"He took and hung it up over the pit. From the vegetable scale." Judiciously, Nathan paused until Buddy's work had resumed rhythm.

"I knew then. I didn't say nothing, I just waited to see. But I knew in my belly from that day. A two-headed monkey was not going to bring him no luck."

60

AND NATHAN SAID:

"She came through with a fellow from Denton, the first time. She had this yellow hair and these smoke-colored eyebrows and she wasn't no bigger than four foot eleven. She was wearing this gray dress, look like it was cut from a prison shirt. But it hung on her just like a ninety-cent negligee, was what he said. That was after her and the Denton fellow had gone on, and I could see from his eyes what come next. The idea of her was still in there, burnt like a cigarette smudge on his brain.

"The Denton man told a story about how he was driving her back down to his sister's, in San Antone. She was his sister's girl, the man said. And she had been up with him and the wife for a visit. Now he was taking her home. He explained it all through like that, two or three times, while she snooped and pouted along up and down the snake cages. And I guess I was the only one there to believe what he said. Later she told us, when she come back, that the man had been principal of her reform school, up there in Denton. He had stepped out on his wife and his two little boys, she claimed, to take the bolt with her. They decided to do it, she said, that very day whiles he was driving her in his car over to the far side of town, so she could see the nurse. But I never knew whether that story of hers was the truth, any more than his. He looked to me like a drummer.

"She told us her name was Bunny.

"She got almost to Nuevo Laredo with the Denton man, she told us, and then his car blew a tire. He pulled up flat just within eyeshot of this truckstop on the highway, she said, and then commence to curse and dig after his jack. Why don't you drive on up and have the man fix it, she said. No, he said, he would do it himself. It was a hundred and five out there on the highway if it was daylight, she told us. So she said to him she was going to cross over and walk up to the truckstop for a cold drink. And he said, That's right, Honey-bunny, you do that, and he give her two bits.

"And her with nothing at all in her mind but just a cold drink, she told us, till she come up to the truckstop. But then she saw that silver-blue diesel truck pulling away from the pumps, headed back north. And so she stuck out her thumb. That was all, she said, I didn't think about nothing. I just took a notion, and stuck out my thumb. And when she passed by the Denton man, high up in her silver-blue cab, he looked up from his rusty lug nuts, and his jaw fell down like a ham. She just gaped right back at him, straight in the eye, she told us. And didn't neither one of them even wave.

"But when they come back through Bromfuss, and there was the serpentarium sign, she told the trucker to leave her off. She just took a notion again, she guessed. And he said, That's right, you just took you a notion. But then he asked her, did she know why? And her eyes went out to the side and she stood on one leg by the turnstile and looked at the ceiling. She stretched her arms out behind her, like she would do. And she said: 'I ain't never seen no two-headed monkey before.'

"And from that day he lived with her like man and wife, right there in the Gulf and Chicago sleeper car. It was almost a month before I knew what was what. Then I understood. One day I just stopped in my tracks out there by the pit, holding a pail in my hand, and understood. So I thought I would have to run off again, because of my momma, back up in Waco. But I didn't know, run off to where.

"Because I tell you truthfully, I was not so quick. I could

not do for myself. All's I could do was see the bad coming. And I watched it come.

"Now this man was the hardware storekeeper from back there in Bromfuss, the very same one that had sold him his chickenwire. He was six feet and more tall and he weighed about two hundred sixty-five pounds and had a belly on him that hung way out over his belt like a short-order cook or a sheriff. But this man was righteous. On Sunday he was a deacon down at the Baptist assembly, and he had a righteousness on him as big around as his belly. He was the biggest righteous man I ever have seen. He would come out of his store on the street there in Bromfuss, and hold a man's automobile up with his back while the man changed a tire, and not take a cent for it, they said. But I never seen him do that. So I don't know if he took a cent for it or not. He sold six-a-penny nails and adzes and bobwire and Bibles. It was him that spoke up about Bunny.

"It wasn't him that started the thinking about Bunny and us, I expect, nor the talking. There was others for that. It don't need a hardware store man like a blacksmith with the morals of Moses to begin rumoring. But it was the hardware store man that spoke up.

" 'Cause they would leave me behind to look after the turnstile, and hitch them a ride into Bromfuss for beans and bacon and fun. Just about every two weeks, he always had done that, hitched himself in, and he would go on a Monday, and be back before nightfall. But that was before she come out there with us. After she come, and she heard the words 'going to town,' she taken the notion she would like to go too.

"And at first he said, No you ain't either, and he went on by himself. She would sniffle and whine at him, and say how wasn't there a roadhouse down there in Bromfuss, or a cafe or just a bowling parlor maybe, that they could go to and have her some fun? And he told her no, that Bromfuss was just a Baptist feedstore town, and there wasn't no fun to be had. All's there was to be had in Bromfuss, he said, was bacon and beans and chickenwire. And the Baptist folks down in Bromfuss didn't believe in no fun, he told her. What they believed in was chickenwire. He said just she should wait, and he would go in and come back, and then they would make their own fun. But she said, Well anyway, Abner, I can't sit out here and stare at a two-headed monkey the rest of my life, now can I? So he took her.

"They went in the morning and wasn't back before dawn the next day. I don't know if they found her a roadhouse or just sat out front the feed store drinking Nehi and watching horse-plop cook in the street. She went along with him to Bromfuss from then on, and they never got back before dawn the next day. And not only that: they taken to going on Saturday.

"But one day it seems this hardware store man said a word to him. It was not a harsh word, most likely. Most likely the hardware store man just drew him off to the side, when he come in there for hinges or wire or carpet tacks, and told him a quiet word as to what folks was thinking. Folks was thinking that she was a pretty young gal for a man like him, I expect, and them not even married. Folks might of heard she was run off from that reform school up in Denton. So the hardware store man might of said a word as to how the whole town was wondering, when did he figure to send her back up to Denton, back up to her people or whoever. I don't know. I don't know what the hardware store man said, 'cause I wasn't nowhere around. But a Saturday hardware store full of folks heard what he said back to the man.

"He let off such a foul filthy spittle of language, I guess, that the very air of the hardware store went sour as heat lightning. Folks lost count of their change and just turned round to stare. He used words that most Bromfuss folks only knew about. But then more. When he had the hardware store man cussed down one side and up the next, for minding the wrong business, he did more. Right there in the man's store, before Saturday customers, he made talk of the hardware storekeeper's wife, and his children. He took reference about the hardware store man's intentions. You married ones with yer kids, he told the hardware storekeeper, you married ones was the worst, when it come to young gals and purity. You married ones was the worst friend a young gal could get. And he had him a reform school principal from up in Denton, he said, to prove it. Folks thought the hardware storekeeper would crack his neck with a pick handle, I guess.

"But the man did not move a finger. The hardware store man just stood and took what he said, and his neck going thick and stiff like cement. The man did not answer back. The man just told him to get out of the store, and so they did.

"He did not take her along to Bromfuss no more after that. He did not go to Bromfuss much more himself. I guess folks still expected the hardware store man must have to split his head with a hame pretty soon, righteous or not. And maybe he thought the same too. But that didn't happen. This other happened instead. And so he lit out with Bunny, and left his shed and his sleeper cars and his whole serpentarium behind, and he did not get a cent for all of his snakes. And he never went back near the town of Bromfuss, so far as I know.

" 'Cause the hardware store man got himself bit by a diamondback.

"And while his wife went across for the doctor, the man's heart up and stopped. Nobody knew why. It just stopped.

"So he opened all of his cages, and then lit out with Bunny, is what I was told later. I don't know for sure how it was, not being there at the time. I only heard how it was, with the hardware store man and all that, much later on. I wasn't around when the two of them got back from town.

" 'Cause when he went into Bromfuss that day, and Bunny along with him, and left me to look after the turnstile, I had taken a notion. I was standing back by the pit with a tin box of mice in my hands, and I just suddenly taken it. So I set down that box of mice where it was, and walked out front to the highway, and stuck out my thumb. I must of stood right on that spot for the best part of four hours. And it was a hundred and five out there, if it was daylight.

"Then the Mexican man in the lettuce truck pulled off to stop. And he was heading all the way up to Wichita, Kansas."

THE CLIFFSIDE STAIRWAY was finished, and Buddy had set to work on the bog: cutting peat. Spread out before the shack in a soft yellow-green oval, the bog was in fact a small pond eaten over by a thick soggy trampoline of peat. Buddy harbored a dream that, once cleared, it might support trout. And anyway, he needed the labor.

He was using a long-handle turf knife to slice away square yards of peat, then dragging each square to shore. He had built racks of aspen on which the peat would be sun-dried for fuel. As Buddy struggled another limp square into place on a rack, Nathan sat near, watching each movement.

Nathan's mood had gone snappish when Buddy first started cutting peat; then settled into a sullen, nervous pout. He had shuffled his old bones up the cliffside, but he would not follow Buddy onto the bog. He seemed to distrust it utterly. Now he would not even resume his recitation while Buddy paused for lunch. Evidently he was that much the egotistical ham, disdaining to perform between interruptions. But the forced silence, the deprivation, was making him edgy. Nathan suffered manifestly as though each yard of harvested peat was an inch of his own skin.

"Hard nasty work. Slow work," Nathan editorialized. They were eating cold rice with scallions; Buddy had never yet refused Nathan food. "Quick as it grows back, fellow can't hardly cut fast enough just to stay even." Buddy sat collapsed in the shack doorway, gasping down mouthfuls.

"How long have you known this piece of land, Nathan?"

"Forty-five years."

"And how much bog was there forty-five years ago?"

"Some. Not a lot. Covered eight, ten feet on this side. Most of the far cove."

"Then I can do better than stay even. If it's taken forty-five years to come this far, I can beat it. You watch. I won't need forty-five years. Sure as you owned a pond here then, I'll own a pond here again."

"You own nothing."

"I own this land. I own the dirt you're sitting on." Buddy flourished his fork. "This. All of it. Me."

"You don't know what you own."

"Welcome to my property, Nathan. Welcome to the future site of Coop's Pond."

"Yes," Nathan said. "I know I am. I been here the whole time."

AND NATHAN SAID:

"Down there in California, he killed a man. Not snakebite nor magic nor ignorant gossip now. I'm talking about what he did with his two hands. It was a poker-game scuffle, and the fellow died.

"I had been gone out of his reach then for six years. And in them six years, I had come up to being a man. First thing he said to me: 'Nathan, there's been some trouble down south, and the fool died.'

"I said to him: 'Where is she?'

"'Where is who?'

"I said: 'Where is yer trouble?'

"Because he knew I had land. Lord knows where he heard. Lord probably even knows how he run up here and put his finger on me, after six years, but I don't. Just one day he was out front the barbershop and the hardware down in Ashland, asking folks did they know of a Texas boy name of Nathan Buckle. Well, that found me, easy enough. It was '37. I had been two years on a tennis-court gang with the WPA, out of Sacramento.

"Tennis courts? Shoot, down there in California we dug so many tennis courts, they couldn't teach folks fast enough how to play the game. So they took us up here into Oregon and give us a mountain to dig. We brung the road in through the pass. Then the gang went off cutting and digging to Portland, but I lingered around over this notion of free government land.

"That's right, land that is yers for the taking, they said, alls you need is to make improvements. I asked them, 'What did a man do to improve a hunk of God's land?' 'Build a shithouse on it,' they said. Well, heard that and I marched up into the hills and hammered together this shack. Forty-five years of dry shelter, but I banged it up in a week. Hardwood, that's why, and you won't find a splinter of pine in it.

"He said: 'Oh, Bunny. Yeah, I expect she'll be along presently. When she take a notion.' He didn't lie then. 'So you got a place of yer own, Nathan?' he said. 'What are you farming, boy?'

"I told him: 'It's planted in muskrats.'

"Because a muskrat is just a creature that loves to be wet. Give him free lunch and a comfortable swamp, you know his address. I started with four breeders, cheaper than seed corn. Built them a nice little pen down the bank here, half into the water and half out, and just every two or three days I put oats in a trough. End of the first year I carried eighty good pelts into town. Not a business to make you rich, but it got me along, and I had my own piece of honest-God paying land. And then him.

"'Muskrats,' he said. 'Muskrats. Well, ain't that fine. Sure. Cart them down into San Francisco and we'll sell them for mink.'

"I said: 'You won't cart shit to a privy.'

"'Remember yer manners, boy,' and he cracked me across the face. Right there on the street, where I did my buying and trading and had the man cut my hair. 'This is yer papa talking to you.' I waited and let him get that off his chest and then I knocked him down. He weren't a big man. I helped him back up.

"'You been six years away,' I said. 'If you wanted some more of them kind of manners, you come about four years too late.'

"He stayed up here near a month before Bunny got more tired of what-all or who-all than she was tired of him. Meantime he was sulky. He pouted around quiet, behaving himself but not real cheerful, not helping with none of my muskratting chores, eating my beans and my bacon. He was hiding away from the poker-game trouble down at Bakersfield, but that was the same to me. It wasn't my trouble, I figured. I didn't care to know nothing about it.

"Here's what he told me: some fool of a man in a white linen suit thought to cheat him of three hundred dollars. Fellow wore straw shoes and had gray on his temples and a razor-slit mustache, and carried his own eyeshade. And a white linen suit that you could not of bought outside New Orleans or for less than a hundred dollars. This fellow was too old for a dandy and too thin for a congressman, as I heard, but he looked to belong on a riverboat. I guess he was just a stocks lawyer out on bail. Well, a fellow that carries his own eyeshade is liable to try anything in a poker game, true enough.

"It was a smoker-car game out of Searchlight, Nevada. He called the cheat and they had a sociable ruckus and he drew a piece of loser's luck. The New Orleans man took a crick in his neck somehow, or something. Weren't any question of pistols or knives, so he claimed, just a clean friendly mix-it-up over three hundred dollars and a pair of bent queens. That's all right. I know myself how they happen. I've seen it.

"Him and Bunny made twenty miles walking through desert before sunrise the next morning. All right. Some folks are not understanding about these poker-game accidents. But I know how they happen. I seen enough for that. Because there's more ways to hit a man than he will ever wake up from. Just 'cause you knock a man upside his ear don't mean you better count on the rascal to stay healthy and tap you one back. There's people die every day of a bee sting and the croup. And a man in straw shoes who will carry his own eyeshade, he's liable to pull anything."

"Probably clubbed him to death with that old brass-head cane," Buddy said.

Nathan studied his face. They both turned to their food. Nathan chewed at the cold rice and swallowed and stared across for another full minute before saying:

"And you'd have me to think that you ain't been paying attention."

"I WANT YOU to listen," Nathan begged.

And then Nathan said:

"I don't know to this day how he kept her. He weren't clever to hear him talk, nor a very good-looking man. He weren't soft with a woman. For fact, he was ornery in the way only a stupid man can be that ornery. And God knows she had a looseness of eye. Maybe she wanted them ornery. Maybe no other man never showed her a two-headed monkey noosed up from a vegetable scale. Well, he kept her six years. Kept her right to the day he died, except for that last month.

"Yes, she was along presently. Come in a orange jeep with some fellow, and walked the last mile. All right, that gives you two grown men and a unmarried gal up here alone in the mountains, living out of a eight-by-eight wood shack. You got the riverboat smartie dead down at Bakersfield. You got nine dozen head of muskrat yet to be harvested. It is November. Now.

"I was contracted with a fellow for cutting a stand of timber, down below over that hill. I had a crosscut and a borrowed mule and I was hauling logs out to the fire road. The fellow give me fifty-five dollars the thousand-foot. The muskrats could look after theirselves. She come, and I took my bedroll and slept in the open. I give them the shack, that I had hammered up with my own hands. It was a plank bunk and a cookstove in there, just like now, and a bare wire bedframe. I slept here by the fire hole. Heard voices awhisper and shouting and left them to do what they would do. Just stirred up early and went off to my stand. I thought he was likely to take and clear her on out.

"First week or two it was, 'Abner, c'mon now, let's get along from here. I don't guess I can spend the rest of my life watching him fuss with them badgers.' She called them badgers. She knew they was muskrats. 'Let's get along up to Portland now, like you said. I don't guess I can spend the rest of my life out here in nowhere just 'cause some fool pair of straw shoes down at Bakersfield tipped over and pointed their toes at the moon. C'mon now.' And he would say, 'Yes, uh-huh. Presently.' Seems he had promised about taking her on up to Portland. 'We'll go when things get all good and quiet,' he said. 'Can't hardly get things more quiet than two Buckle men and a pond full of badgers,' she said. 'It's cold up here. Let's go.' He said, 'Yes, Honeybunny, presently,' and they stayed.

"So I was working a log up to the fire road, in back of that mule. And first thing, I saw her from here to that cross trail of yers, hundred yards off, standing and watching me. She had on a little rag dress and she was holding herself at the elbows to keep warm. I could not make out her face but I could tell she was watching, the way you can tell when the thing that a far-off person is watching is you. I unhitched and went down for another log and drove it back up and she was still watching. I went again and drove up another and she was gone. Next morning she come back and sat on a stump and said, 'You and that mule fixing to drag them all the way down into town?'

"I said no. We wasn't fixing to do that at all. A man would come by in his truck.

"She said: 'Um.'

"I hitched up another and the mule jerked and I very near to had my foot smashed. Went, and come back, and she said: 'Don't you never get tired?' So I quit for a drink from the pail, and wet my face.

"She said: 'How old are you, Nathan?'

"I said: 'Twenty years.'

"She said: 'Me, I'm a old woman of twenty-two.'

"I said: 'Yes, ma'am.'

"And she said: 'Did you ever touch a old woman, Nathan?'

"I said: 'Yes, ma'am. I have. Down there in Sacramento. Had me a five-dollar woman this one time. Must of been forty years old if she was weaned.'

"She said: 'Nathan, you come over here, boy.'

"So I set down the ladle and walked back to that mule and snapped it across the flank with them lines and I said: 'Up!'

"Three days, nothing more. Then he took a notion of going down into town. 'And I am too,' she said. But he said: 'No you ain't either. We seen how that come out already before. Just bring you along to town and some hardware store Moses will get himself bit with a snake. No thank you.' He told her he wasn't going to town for no fun. He was going to smell out the air, he told her. And maybe then they could get along up to Portland. I heard all they was saying from outside the shack here. She said: 'Yes, and then whose fault is it gonna be when that boy of yers has me off in the weeds?' He didn't say nothing to that, not for some time. Then he commenced to laugh. She did not laugh. They both knew I was out here, in earshot, awake on the ground. Next morning he walked into town.

"Hauled logs all that day and she sat on a stump and we didn't have two words for each other. Fixed a supper and left it for her on the stove. She could eat it if she had the notion. Nighttime, and she stuck her head out to say, 'You might as well sleep in the shack if you want. It's just a empty bunk here. Might as well you be in it as empty.' I slept on the dirt and it dribbled a cold November rain. Covered my head with a sheet of rubber, and I guess I slept just as good as any man does who is sleeping wet. Next day the same, but she did not offer no invitations. Just slammed herself up inside the shack. Third day, still the cold dribble, and that mule could not get a good footing, so I cut timber and left it lay. Come up at night, and there he was back.

"He had brought whiskey. He seem to have spent a good part of his town time hooked over the rim of a glass. He was frisky and chirpy in the way such a ornery man as him will not do when he has all his sober wits. He was not much a drinking man, and now he was getting him drunk. All right, I thought to myself then. All right. Well, the air smelled friendly enough, he said, and he guessed it had come time they could get along up to Portland, he said. Tomorrow, or maybe the next day, whichever. She wasn't saying too much of nothing. Asked me for two glasses and they shut the shack door in my face and lit my kerosene lamp. I went to bed on the muck, third night in a row. Half hour or a hour went by quiet before I woke up and heard their ruckus.

"She was squalling and sobbing like a fat woman in the opera. Heard her scream: 'Yes, and whose fault is that then, Mister Go-to-town? Leave me alone here with nothing but that boy of yers, full-grown buck man, and a hundred square miles of bushes, and what else did you expect? Who warned you already before?' Heard that, and yes I felt cold rain.

"My daddy hollered: 'He never!'

"She hollered: 'No, that's right, he would never of knowed how!' and then more of her crying. 'But what else did you expect?'

"My daddy: 'He never! Nathan? He never!'

"Her: 'Well then what am I squalling about, Abner?'

"Took my bedroll and went stumbling down to the cutting stand where I couldn't hear them, and went back to sleep under that sheet of rubber. I was thinking that if they would only just get up in the morning and lit off, get on up to Portland, then maybe I would never see neither of them ever again. I hoped they would do it. I went off to sleep thinking that, and thinking just one other thing: that old twelve-gauge I had laying up in the shack.

"Well, I heard him before he got within twenty yards. Slipping and thrashing down through the brush and groaning my name like a longhorn. I didn't know if it was nighttime or early morning, but it was dark yet. And that cold rain. Not making a whisper of sound, I reached for the axe that I kept there for limbing. I waited, laying up next to a deadfall, under that dark sheet of rubber, till he everything but stepped right down on me.

"So I got a look at the barrel of that twelve-gauge before ever I saw him. Come out over me like the snout of some wicked animal sniffing blood, and then him. I left him to take three steps beyond. I swear it to you and to God overhead and I'll swear the same thing to any man, that I only thought of getting that twelve-gauge away from him, and then I would unload it. I swear that to you just as I'm sitting here. And if you don't believe it of me, then what you believe is a lie. I thought of no thought but just getting that gun, so I could unload it. Waited. He staggered on drunk a few steps moaning 'Nathaaan!' and I come out with the dull side of that axe.

"Took him across the back of the kneecaps like he was wheat. I got a hand on that gun but he was back at me, snarling like a wolverine. There in the dark, he did not sound more than half human.

"I yanked that shotgun around thinking to crack open the breech, and him clawing and grabbing and biting to get back ahold of it, and me jabbing my elbow into his face till I could feel and hear his teeth ripping loose, and then he had a grip of it, by the barrel. He was a small man, but strong. He frightened the life out of me when he hooked onto that shotgun. He was not saying a human word. Nor neither was I. I jerked back on the stock; then thunder. I blew his kneecap right off the leg.

"I said: 'Daddy!'

"And he said: 'Yes, Nathan. Awwhh. Yes, boy.'

"I got him up to the shack, and it was light now, and she was gone. Never saw her again, to this day. She never come back around asking for him, nor even to learn what happened, so far as I know. Heard that shot, and it was enough. I had killed him or he had killed me, either way. I guess she just wasn't curious. And her off somewhere now a woman of sixty-some-odd years old, if the Lord wills it. Ain't that a picture. And did she ever know what become of him, after six years of the two of them? No she did not. I can tell you she did not. Not her, nor no one else.

"Wrapped the leg up with a piece of my shirt, down there in the dark of the stand, and carried him up here to the shack. When light broke I seen that the kneecap was gone, it was just gone, like the top smashed off a mason jar full of raspberry jam. His kneecap was back down on the ground somewhere, at the stand, or it was just scattered everywhichway. I set to go for a doctor. But he said no.

"He would not have me go for no doctor. I will not tell you why because I don't know why. He claimed it was on account of the straw shoes down at Bakersfield, but that was only a lie. He had other reason. I don't say what it was. I don't know. Sometimes I have thought I knew why he did it. But that was wrong. I don't know why.

"He said 'That's all right, Nathan, you can do all the doctoring I'm gonna need. It ain't so bad. I'll tell you how to do, boy.' It was not a deep wound, for a gunshot, but it was a dread ugly hash of a hole. 'Now dump some hot water over that thing and then let's get it back out of sight under that rag. It's all right, boy.'

"Lingered along almost a month till he died. His knee festered and stunk just like his hand stunk from that diamondback, and he went through a fever. I knew the stink of my daddy's dying flesh, in that little shack. Snow come then, and it was cold for us in there. First snow, but it come with a hard cold snap and lasted a week. We could not keep his leg warm, not with a flaring cookstove nor blankets nor hot cobbles. Because he could not move that leg. So the blood in that leg lay down and stopped where it was, and the leg died, and taken to going colors. Then it did not stink no more. We were too cold up here for flesh to stink. I want to tell you, that leg was a mess.

"I said: 'I'm going to town. I'm going, and bring back a doctor. I'm scared for that leg to rot right off yer body, and you'll die.'

"He said: 'No you ain't either.'

"And I said: 'But I am,' and I left. Got half a mile off in the snow till I heard that twelve-gauge again. I came hopping back in a hot sweat but he was still there, on the bare wire bedframe. He hadn't done nothing. He had just fired a round into the door, and blowed the door off its hinges.

"He said: 'See if you bring a doctor for me.' He said: 'And next time you go off, Nathan, don't just think of taking the shells. Take all the knives and ropes too. See if you get me a doctor.'

"So I did not. I stayed right in that shack with him, watching my daddy rot. Then he died. The last three or four days he fevered again, and did not say nothing. He did not tell me no good-byes. He did not tell me nothing. He just died. He had what he wanted.

"Twenty inches of snow, and the ground frozen like stone.

I sat up with him inside there for two days, after he died, not doing nothing but stay just warm enough to keep me alive. I did not know what to do. He was a man I did not like, but he was my daddy, and now I had killed him. And now it was mine to bury him. I could not leave him be, for the vermin and animals. I could not put him into the ground.

"I took and tied him right down to that bedframe with rope, tied his two hands and his two feet and tied him around the middle. I dragged him and that bedframe out of the shack and right down through here to the pond, it was still a pond then, and right out across that ice I dragged him and pushed him, plowing two feet of snow along as I went. I scooped out a space from the snow. And then I took that same axe I had used when I cut him down, and hacked me a hole.

"And you know what I done with him then but I'm going to tell you the rest anyway. Lined up with that smaller of two firs on the far side. You see? Right across here. About midway from this side to the other." Nathan was unrelenting. "You see?"

By the firelight Buddy saw only Nathan, pointing toward the bog. Beyond in the darkness he could discern no pair of firs, but he knew they were there. Buddy sat very still, chilled by the ice of a long-passed winter, chilled with recognition, moving only to shiver.

He knew there was more. He knew that both liens were being called, and that his mountain hideout was already in foreclosure.

"I chopped me a hole in that ice, big enough for a man and a bedframe," Nathan said. "And then I buried my daddy through it. Sunk him right out of sight."

℘ Uriah's Letter ℘

I

Imagine it. You open to the first page and immediately there is this swamp-hatched, obsessive delivery:

From a little after the Negro boy appeared with the old woman's message of summons, until well past suppertime, Henry Graham sat in rapt unflinching incomprehension on the breezeless wicker-jalousied gallery of the house—more like a sun-exposed prison cell than a porch, with its yellow slashes of trapped heat slicing acute through the blinds, perhaps more like some child's inhumane cricket cage left out in the afternoon than either—before the hard straight chair from which Miss Louisa's legs hung rigid and plumb as brass pendulums, clear of the floor, just as her faint unhurried relentless hard voice came at him, flagged and transmuted yet forever unchanged like the greened-over bronze of the courthouse dome, coming out of the old time, the old wrong, the old rage now twenty-eight years impacted beneath the memory of that long-absent object of her sustaining if bootless vindiction, until at last Henry's hearing-act would yield and surrender itself as her recounting-act did to the very act-less and inhuman and irrepressible momentum of the story itself, the faded bloodied proscenium and the cruel props and the characters of the dress-drama, and amid them that single overscale demon-like actor, the source and the object of her bitterness, abrupting upon the scene out of no footlights but the dreamy and silent and gore-darkened dust of the War, *you read.*

What? you ask. Come again?

The voice would not halt, it would merely recede, remove beyond harkening through the curtain of scenery itself had evoked, the night shadows breaking across fires laid out in a pine grove and the anonymous weary murmur of infantry bivouac. And Henry now from his seat on the porch in long moments of entranced credulity that seemed even to him like remembering would look on as General Joe Johnston with four fresh divisions stood off between Grant and the city of Jackson, waiting—waiting for what, only Joe Johnston knew. This much was indeed memory, by transpiration not recollection since he, Henry, listening here in 1913, had been born to and still breathed the same Mississippi air in which those bivouac fires had burned just fifty years earlier through the seven lingering summer weeks of a city's ordeal. These names were familiar to him, not as names but as people, as progenitors, as the thickener to that stout bitter broth he had been fed on his eighteen years, pride and intransigence and pride again: Joe Johnston, the man who delayed; Stuart, Forrest, the unfortunate Earl Van Dorn; Bragg and Beauregard; and the Pennsylvanian, Pemberton. The place was familiar to Henry also, with its steep wooded hills and its redoubts and its trenches, and the city that lived behind walls with its back to a river, familiar too not as a place (which he had never actually visited, though it was less than a half day by train) but as an idea for times and minds, as an hour of the heart: Vicksburg. The place and the men were familiar, and Henry would see them, in the dark of a June evening fifty years gone, bent over map tables to the sepia shimmer of a tent lit by kerosene. The soldiers too, pickets chilled beyond reach of the fires, others slumbering or cursing quietly for their own amusement nearer the circle, scabrous red-browns of battle pentimentoed behind the tidier black-yellow of night. But it was not to these men nor this place that the voice of Louisa Sterne drew him. Returning by and by to the foreground of Henry's attention, that voice was insistent, was askew, was embattled in skirmish of its own with the very memory evoked. "His name was Surrat," said the voice. "He was staff colonel to Joe Johnston. But he was a man without honor," *you read.*

"Yessum," Henry said. But *why me?* he thought. *Why tell me about it?*

Why indeed? you think. Why any of us? But you are, say, a patient soul. And so you read on.

"Now you will leave us here soon, I am informed, to go up to the college at Harvard," Miss Louisa addressed Henry. "So you will be living and schooling with Yankees and Jews perhaps and the sons of the very men who have seen to it that there is so little left in the South that a young man of promise must go North to advance himself, and you will be far away from those of your own kind. Nor do I expect you will find reason up there to return to a small town like this. I do not expect even Harvard can teach you that. But perhaps someone among those new friends, the Yankees and Jews and sons of the manufactors and even perhaps scions of foreign courts, some one of them may ask you sometime. 'Tell about the South,' this one may ask. 'What is it like there? How do they live there? Who are they?' Or perhaps not until after you have settled and become a respectable broker of stocks or of cotton in some Northern city, and married North and born children North. Perhaps only then one of your daughters will learn belatedly and with quiet unplumbable wonderment that you her father are in fact of the race Mississippian born and nurtured, and then she will ask: 'What is the South? Where is it? How do they live there? And why?' So you will be thankful perhaps then to the old woman who once detained you for all of a long hot September afternoon with talk of war and betrayal and outrage that occurred before you or she either were born. And then, whether that time be sooner or later, you will remember at least something. And you will have this to tell."

"Yessum," Henry said. Only that ain't the reason, he thought. Only what is?

The summoning note was still in his pocket, delivered by hand of the small Negro boy just before noon, a message unexpected, inexplicable and out of another world—which he nevertheless promptly obeyed—in the faint formal pen scratches of a woman thirty years his senior whom he had known all his life as a familiar but distant feature of the landscape, yet with whom he had exchanged no more than a few sentences ever before this afternoon. A furious, abstract and slightly awry incarnation of womanhood, this woman, more ghost than lady and more anomaly than ghost: a Northern-bred girl herself, who came South to marry and did not marry and stayed South and despised it, who nursed an indefinite grudge for some twenty years, only to recant and reverse at the last and nurse on his deathbed the very man against whom the grudge had been held, the Old Governor, Joseph Surrat. (Yes, Henry knew the name well. It too was an ingredient of the air he breathed, the broth he was fed.) Then to resume after that man's death more vehement than even previously the impacted unapproachable bitterness: this Miss Louisa Sterne.

But does she really want me to hear it? Henry thought. Or does she herself just want to get shut of it? And why, he thought, did she choose of all people me?

Listening, Henry wondered.

Correct, he thought, I don't even know that, *you read.*
And now, God knows, you might sit back to clear your head.

⁓

BUT STILL the woman's voice comes at you. She talks. In a continuous mad rapture of language, her soliloquy flows through the long afternoon—Henry's long afternoon, and your own. Except for Henry's Yessums, his No'me, the speech is uninterrupted. A patient soul, say, you read on.

And learn that she was obsessed with the Old Governor, this Joseph Surrat. Of a later generation, unrelated by blood or marriage, she was evidently never close to him. Her interest in the full sweep of his life seems perfunctory. But she dwells upon him, upon one side of his character, upon what she portrays as his furtive nature, as though to find explanation there for the barrenness of her own life. The man performed some single act by which was set, so she believes, her destiny. Though she makes oblique reference to it repeatedly throughout the chapter, Miss Louisa refrains from stating just what this act could have been. The narrator's voice calls it the impacted source of her rage. Meanwhile her words swarm on through the thick humid air, gathering like excited insects around the figure of Joseph Surrat.

To Hadrian, Mississippi, Surrat came south from Kentucky, at the close of 1849. He arrived alone and on horseback, a young quiet man about twenty with no distinction of bearing. His dark broadcloth coat was tastefully cut but threadbare; it was clean. His entrance was not memorable. The fact of his presence became known to the townspeople only gradually. He took a place at a rooming house on the far outskirts of town kept by a Mrs. James, wife to the man who ran the local livery business. No one understood, no one bothered to wonder, why this young man had chosen Hadrian. And Joseph Surrat himself didn't say.

Early evidence, Miss Louisa implies, of his secretiveness.

Later some would believe Surrat the son of a wealthy Kentucky planter of tobacco. He had left home or been driven off, they would say, with only the good clothes he wore and his fine white-stockinged roan, after an irreconcilable falling-out with his father. It involved the death of a brother, some claimed to know. Or possibly, there had been a dispute over money. Whatever, the young man left, and rode south only so far as Hadrian.

At other times, the same folk would swear that Joseph Surrat was no more than the youngest whelp of a Kentucky hill-country sharecropper, and that they had known this truth all along, despite his pretensions. The coat had come second-hand from a beneficent lawyer in Nashville. Or perhaps it was stolen. He had struck an impression of gentility, they decided, simply by his quietness.

This Joe Surrat lived for one year in the James boarding-house, found work with the railroad on a line then being built down from Memphis, kept to himself. His days he spent with the section gang, his evenings alone in his room, and on Sunday he was sometimes seen walking the streets of town, silent, preoccupied. He spoke to few people besides his hostess, her husband, and their young son Uriah. He took his meals with the family. He had not known hard labor before, Mrs. James thought, because after four days on the section his hands had blistered and broken to open sores. Surrat allowed her to wrap them for him in rags soaked with warm vinegar. But he did not complain, and stayed at the work until he was comfortable with it.

After a year, he was suddenly gone. He no longer appeared with the James family on Sunday for Methodist worship. When asked, Mrs. James explained that he was now living in Oxford, the college town, thirty miles east. Given the opportunity to read for the bar in the office of a lawyer there, he had accepted and left immediately. So the townspeople now realized, or assumed, that Joseph Surrat had in fact been a man of some education, before coming to Hadrian. A few said that the Oxford lawyer was a business connection of Mr. James, whose wife had pressed him to arrange the apprenticeship. Mr. James himself had once admitted that his wife seemed the only person in Hadrian who could quite understand young Joe Surrat. Other folks heard differently, that the Oxford man was a friend of Surrat's own father, up in Kentucky. This suggested that the dispute responsible for Surrat's exile, from his home, from his class, had been resolved. Whichever, Hadrian residents did not now expect they would ever see Joseph Surrat again.

After three years, he rode back into Hadrian, a lawyer. He seemed nearly as reticent as before, but with some slightly increased sense of purpose and confidence. Again he put up at the James boardinghouse. When he rented a small second-floor office over the square, had his name lettered onto the window and sat down at a bare desk to wait, the townsfolk were puzzled. Surrat had no people in Hadrian, they knew. He had no friends there, they believed. His earlier life must certainly still lie in wreckage, they thought, if he could find no better place to settle. Some guessed that Mrs. James had become more of a mother to him than the Kentucky planter's wife ever had been. Joseph Surrat did not supply the answer.

That was his way, Miss Louisa inserts. He did things with hidden purposes: more hidden than those of most men. She still to this day cannot say why he chose Hadrian.

Finally a few climbed the stairs, and allowed Surrat to practice some law. They found him a good advocate who worked hard out of court and studied his books and got up his cases thoroughly, winning as often as not. He was never a courtroom orator. Sometimes he stood silent before the bench or in front of a jury for two or three minutes together, his expression as empty and slack as when he had first ridden into town, while he searched for a word or a thought. But people trusted his effort, they trusted his plodding studiousness, Miss Louisa says, because he never gave them a chance to do otherwise.

He was always smarter than they judged him, she says. That was their mistake. That was the measure of his cunning.

Now he made friends, but not easily, and not many. There were a few men with whom he hunted, one a fellow lawyer, one the town schoolteacher, one Mr. James of the livery business. He took a drink, but he didn't gamble, and he didn't go to Memphis for women. Occasionally he still attended the Methodist church with Mrs. James and Uriah. He remained an indifferent bachelor. Sometimes he would be invited out to one of the big houses for a social evening with young ladies, and sometimes he went. He was polite and conversable, but never quite charming. People of Hadrian came to accept and then largely forget his presence among them, even the mothers of marriageable daughters, simply because Joseph Surrat was not an interesting man about whom to think. He seemed to have passed from extreme youth, as when they first saw him, directly into late middle age. Most of his free hours were spent with the boy, Uriah.

Uriah was devoted to this quiet man just eleven years his elder. During the earlier stay, Uriah had been a bright open child of nine. They had grown to be friends, and on leaving for Oxford, Joseph Surrat had given Uriah his first adult rifle. Uriah was now a good hunter, an excellent rider. Growing up in his father's stables, he had known and tended and sat upon horses since he could walk. He loved to ride. As a boy of ten and eleven, he would ride far out into the pine woods west of Hadrian, dismount, and hunt until dark in the virgin stands. Struggling through adolescence, he still went to the pine stands, hunting more reverently and prizing the hours more fiercely than ever. And his friend Joseph Surrat began to talk to him as a man.

Then Mr. James died, and so Uriah was a man. Joseph Surrat, an established town lawyer who now lived by himself in a small house he had built off the square, saw Mr. James into the grave. He performed all the arrangements and legal functions of funeral, will, and estate. Uriah was sixteen. Mrs. James sold the stables and carried on with her boarding-house, a strong sensitive woman mortally saddened but unbowed by the loss of her husband. Finished with school, Uriah helped her. Then she also died. Uriah was eighteen.

That year, Uriah began to read law in the office of Joseph Surrat. It was 1859.

Soon after, townspeople noticed that Uriah had begun keeping company once again with a young Hadrian girl he had known since childhood. Her name was Ruth Cullum. She had lately metamorphosed from the small stalky tousle-haired tomboy of earlier days into a small graceful woman. Her hair was light brown, Miss Louisa says, her skin was now pale with womanhood, and on one cheek she bore a birthmark the size of a man's thumbnail and the color of wheat. Uriah had grown up with her for a playmate. In the two years between his father's death and his mother's, he had seemed to forget her. The daughter of a judge, she had spent those two years at the Women's Academy in Oxford. She returned, a Southern lady. She found Uriah a grown man with no family, heir to a large house and forty acres on the out-skirts of Hadrian, himself soon to emerge from apprentice-ship as a lawyer.

In late 1860, they were married. The South Carolina convention passed secession. And then, Mississippi.

Confederate uniforms appeared on the square in the spring of 1861. Judge Cullum was raising an Hadrian regiment. But the first man to leave town for duty was Joseph Surrat. He had obtained a captaincy with the first Confederate Army, in northern Virginia. No one knew how. They could only guess that the family connections from Kentucky must have helped him again, and this vague assumption didn't satisfy them. He closed up the law office and rode east, alone, for service under Beauregard. The town was more jealous than proud.

When the Hadrian regiment finally assembled, Uriah James wasn't with it either. Taking the best bay gelding unsold from his father's business, Uriah had left his young wife in the big house and ridden off to face Yankee armies as a cavalry trooper under Earl Van Dorn. The younger man would never live to practice law, Miss Louisa says darkly, in Mississippi or anywhere else. Though Yankee armies, she says, were the least of what menaced him.

Why wouldn't he live to practice law? What else menaced him? You have no idea what she means. But having followed the old woman this far, say, you read on.

⌒

"So Surrat was with Beauregard at Manassas," Miss Louisa said. "But not Beauregard nor six hundred Beauregards could lend honor to a man without. No, nor Robert E. Lee himself. And Surrat was a man without honor.

"Oh, I claim no pity for Uriah James: blind ingenuous trusting boy with nothing to excuse him but youth and orphanhood and that sickening mortar of epic foolhardy idolatry so common between man and man when subjected to each other's conjuring too long at the wrong time of life, as Uriah had now been subjected since the age of nine. No, blind ingenuous acolyte, then later unblindered helpless victim, to a man pretending friendship and honor and a relation almost of fatherhood, which man would and did play upon twelve years of mutual indebtedness to see off into the muzzle of certain oblivion the boy he had practically helped to raise, and then turn round himself and with aboriginal absence of shame take the other man's wife for his own, not two months after that boy-man was listed as dead.

"Because Uriah deserves none and needs none: pity nor mourning nor sympathy for the loss of wife and homeland and all else there had been to his narrow world and his short life. Because the vengeance was his, as Uriah knew it would be and more even than he could have known. Because vengeance cannot be purchased but once because after the first it is simply bloodlust and rage.

"Yes, Surrat was a man without honor. So he married Ruth James that August, just a month after Vicksburg, less than two months into her widowhood, when the memory of her first husband was not yet dimmed in even the minds of well-wishing strangers about Hadrian. And the good folk of town were amazed and abashed, though they needn't have been. They said nothing, of course. The rumors had already been whispered and heard and repeated about Uriah's own conduct, and the word treason spat into the clear spring of his reputation, and people still had a war not only to win but a Cause to continue believing in. So they quickly preferred to cease thinking about Uriah James, and his wife, and his friend. Surrat married the young widow as swift as a barn snake and as quiet as a knife and left her installed shamelessly in the very James house that had served him his first borrowed roof and hot meal and clean bed in Hadrian. Then he rode back to Johnston, from what seems to have been his second eventful leave home in less than a year. And the son was born. They named him Chamberlain Surrat. Cham.

"So if the townspeople looked and saw something in this gambit more than that earnest and wistful and studious irresoluteness they had told themselves for so many years they were viewing in Joseph Surrat, then they needn't have been surprised," Miss Louisa said.

"No'me," Henry said.

Second eventful home-leave? Rumors of treason? What the devil is she talking about? you wonder.

⁓

YOU READ THAT Surrat returned from the war—defeated and haggard yet like the others unvanquished, as Miss Louisa puts it—to a part of the land merely defeated and haggard, to a town that had been burnt by the cavalry raiders of Grierson. His wife and the two-year-old son were waiting, still in the old boardinghouse with most of its first floor now charred and unliveable from a Yankee torch. Slowly and circumspectly, as he had always done everything, Surrat began to re-establish his law practice in a ruined town. And more: his wife had property now, from her first husband, the traitor, and from her father, who had succeeded at his advanced age in dying valorously from a wound at Chickamauga. Surrat held in her name over sixty acres within the greater limits of Hadrian. He used it, sold not a square foot but parlayed it, as the burned businesses from the square began trying to rise from their ashes. Reconstruction was a windstorm against him. But he prospered. People trusted in him more than ever. He was Colonel Surrat. He had been with Lee.

Twelve years passed before the last Federal troops were withdrawn from the North Mississippi Department. Surrat spent the first six of those years in a sort of discreet domestic retirement out at the large James homestead, now restored, no longer a boardinghouse, with his wife and the growing son. Then with startling bad timing, at age thirty, the wife died of diphtheria. The boy nearly died too, but survived. And now, from this sudden widowerhood, Joseph Surrat emerged into what Miss Louisa with saccharine irony is pleased to call his civic phase.

He began working actively against the powers of occupation: those cynical Northern commercial men who had come down to put illiterate Southern blacks over their old masters, into the courthouse and statehouse and even the Congress, in service of no principle but their own profit, says Miss Louisa. Some believed that during this period Joe Surrat was a night-rider, a leader of those white-hooded former Confederates who occasionally still rose up to lynch a Yankee or burn a barn or a Negro in kerosene. And they were glad to believe it. They had to believe it, says Miss Louisa, because he was their ranking surviving officer. He did not encourage their belief. His outward life remained impeccably civic; he was merely the fussy professional, faintly aloof, dignified in the acceptance of the futility of his labors. But the Union army could not stay forever.

In 1880 Hadrian sent him to the legislature. He took the boy Chamberlain with him, making special arrangements for schooling. After a tumultuous session Joseph Surrat returned to Hadrian thin and morose, but a martyr in the eyes of the town, the lonely widower scarred by war and personal loss, struggling to be father and mother both to a son on the brink of manhood, yet still sacrificing himself in efforts toward the general resurrection. In 1886, riding a great swell of sentiment, his name linked in formula with that of Lee, he declared himself for the Democratic nomination to the Governorship of Mississippi.

And now even the town of Hadrian would realize that Joseph Surrat was not the man they had thought, Miss Louisa says. Only they would tell themselves how much he had changed. Miss Louisa herself, it seems, saw no such change.

But the citizenry, at their distance, were free to speculate. Perhaps the spell of the chamber in Jackson, perhaps the death of his wife, perhaps something as long ago as the war, had begun the change, they would guess. Those who had always doubted his role in the Klan, unable to picture Surrat commanding a posse of murderous rabble, now believed, Miss Louisa says. Joseph Surrat seemed to them neither retiring nor irresolute. Something, during how many years they were not sure, had been growing within him. He had comfortable wealth, position in his community, a grown son, the satisfaction of service well done. He had everything they had thought he possessed the capacity to want. But he wanted more: the Governorship of Mississippi.

He was not drafted, she says. He was not cajoled. He reached out to take it. Power's hunger for power gleamed in the man's eye. The citizenry, Miss Louisa says, needn't have been surprised.

So you aren't surprised either. Duly warned, vigilant, still more than a little mystified, you read on.

"AND YET I CANNOT pretend he surprised me less than the rest," Miss Louisa told Henry. "I would like to, but I cannot. Because I was born too late. I was born three years and a war and one marriage too late.

"Neither do I claim pity myself: blind romantic fool of a girl that I was, not twenty years old and a stranger still to the South and to Southern ways, feverish with love misguided by hope and demented with fear and joy and anticipation. I was a living compoundment of cliché and improbability converging toward irony. I had come South, been sent South, for a lady's education. I had found or believed I had found love. I planned and expected marriage. And I received in the end nothing but education. Yes, I did indeed receive a lady's education.

"Abandoned by my fiancé in the very foyer of marriage, renounced by my father-in-law presumptive, a strange young woman in a small vicious Southern town with no bridal bower to enter beneath nor any home toward which I cared to return, I had nothing but to languish and die then or learn quickly to scrape out my own debased living. Which is what I have done these twenty-eight years, moving no farther than this the scene of my greatest humiliation and disappointment, groveling for my sustenance like a forgotten ewe grazing on stubble and languishing only in what few moments of these twenty-eight years others might have called my spare time. Yet I claim no pity. I deserve none. Because I too, in love with a handsome young man and in love with the idea of love and already gone smug in the soft loveless prospect of comfortable successful marriage, I too had said to myself: All this, and a governorship as well?"

II

IT WAS A SUMMER of wistaria. The vine on its wooden trellis filling one end of the gallery had bloomed for the second time that season, and the soft suspirant breath of early September dusk rising cool up the cedar corridor brought the odor of blossoms to mingle with the scent of Henry's father's pipe, as Henry and Reverend Graham sat on the veranda after their late supper. They were waiting for darkness, when Henry would bring the phaeton around to return for Miss Louisa, and in the meantime Henry's father rested his feet on the white-painted railing and worked with a small tool at lighting and cleaning and packing and re-lighting his pipe in the casual furious absorption that could cause an uninured stranger to scream, and spoke. Henry listened. He had spent and would spend that day listening, to Miss Louisa then his father then Miss Louisa again, when in an hour or two he would reappear for her as promised and escort her in the phaeton across town and out to the Old Governor's vacant house, for what purpose she yet declined to reveal, certain to hear still again, then, of those same names and places and alcohol-pickled glories and outrages which now for the first time seemed to blend in tyrannous olfactory collusion with the wistaria and the tobacco and the summer-dusk to form one smothering odor familiar yet horrible, and Henry wondered, watching the pipe tool's movements, whether it might not now be himself who would scream.

I have been listening too long, he thought. I have heard the story too many times, Henry thought, hearing again the flat leaden knell of that single Methodist church bell ringing out in the same air that was still his, so they said, to breathe, ringing on that Sunday morning of 1849 when the town in assembly had its first glimpse of Joseph Surrat and realized almost at once that he was among them to stay, according to Reverend Graham. This young Surrat was seated dutiful and erect in the pew between Mrs. James, an imperious stout woman whose figure consisted mainly of skirts, and her husband, a gaunt man of quiet demeanor and a visage marked with something the same sad and tepid futility as Lincoln's, according to Reverend Graham.

"Yes, the town didn't know quite what to make of Joe Surrat, I suppose, in those early years. He seemed to be taking his place in Hadrian as though born or anointed to it. Yet he was an outlander." Reverend Graham prodded the bowl of his pipe, letting his mouth corners droop under the weight of irony. "He had come from as far north as Tennessee."

"Tennessee," Henry said. "Miss Louisa told me Kentucky."

"Ah," his father said. "Of course. But it was Tennessee. He may have been born in Kentucky. Probably was. Still, he had lived most of his young life in Nashville. An uncle there, an attorney, had taken him in, after the death of his father.

"I suppose that the mother, perhaps a Tidewater woman, finding herself with a tobacco plantation to run and a full stock of niggers to look after and keep under hand, and then this young boy to be raised, I suppose she had figured herself unequal to the task, and she chose the plantation. I don't know. So she put little Joe out to the lawyer in Nashville, who was her brother. Certainly, it is not ours to judge her for that. Perhaps she saw rightly that a boy over age six needs a father more than a mother even if the father be only an uncle, just as a girl over age ten needs an older sister more than anything else in the world. Perhaps it was even a sacrifice, her relinquishment, to what she saw as the boy's greater good, to his future. Who can say. So he came down to Nashville and grew up a transplant in his uncle's house. And that's where he first started to read law."

"Yessir," Henry said. "How do you know?"

"But the uncle it happened was an older man of stiff shirt fronts and high collars who viewed the law as a religion if not a god and himself as Jonathan Edwards. He was already middle-aged when the sister deposited her boy on his doorstep and had raised two other sons to manhood and the bar and a sort of imbecile junior partnership in his own office before he began with Joe Surrat. So he thought he knew the way it was done. As Surrat matured, he found the lawyer was too much of a father or the uncle found Surrat not enough of a lawyer, and he had to get out. There was no rancor in his departure, but neither was there regret. The uncle's home and the office and perhaps Nashville itself had simply become too small for what Joseph Surrat sensed vaguely were to be the dimensions of his life. So he rode south without plan to the first town whose dogs did not bark at him yet in which he would be a complete stranger.

"He began work with the railroad and meanwhile cast about wondering what he should make of himself. He hated the railroad. From the day he turned out till the day he quit, almost a year later, he hated the work and the idea of railroad work but most of all hated the crude cheerful raucous egalitarianism within which like a sweaty embrace the section gang lived. They bunked in cars out on the siding (except for him, who preferred to ride the white-stockinged roan four miles back and forth each morning and evening) and what few hours of freedom they had between Monday and Saturday were spent in that same coagulant solidarity, drinking and whoring, each man as good as the other and getting no better nor worse. It tortured Surrat, believing as he did that he was indeed too good for it, but unable to say for what he was just good enough. After the year, he brooded a fortnight on the desperate idea of returning to Nashville. But then a man in Oxford came to his rescue: he might continue the law, if he wanted. Well, the law was not what he wanted. But it was what he would take. Impatient with Joe Surrat's confused anguish, Mrs. James had arranged the offer. She had forced her husband to call in a favor."

"Yessir," Henry said. "How do you know?"

"From Uriah," said Reverend Graham. "Your grandfather

told me the story. Your grandfather rode under Buck Van Dorn too, you recall. From Jackson to Pea Ridge to Spring Hill, Tennessee, he rode boot and stirrup beside Uriah James."

"Oh," Henry said. "Yes. I recall."

Reverend Graham brought his feet down from the railing, drawn forward in the chair by his own shifted attention.

"They left town together, in '61, your grandfather and Uriah. Both of them just about twenty years old. Just about your age, give a year or two. Picture it: turning their horses, and that gay callow bellicosity of first manhood, toward Jackson, where Van Dorn was now major general over all Mississippi volunteers. But they knew Earl Van Dorn for a cavalry man, not a field commander (much as you would know Vardaman for a hog farmer) and in that knowledge they founded their expectations. They were to be frustrated and diverted, yes, but not finally denied.

"So they rode to their war, Uriah and your grandfather, self-congratulatory as you can imagine in the macabre if accurate estimate (or perhaps hope) that no more than one of their pair now would ever see peace and old age. Of course, the young wife whom Uriah had kissed at his doorway and then swung himself free of and into the saddle without a look back was in your grandfather's case a properly bumptious mother (your own great-grandmother) sending him off with saddlebags packed full of chicken and biscuits and an egregious supply of clean linen and instructions not to be overly impatient of getting himself killed.

"They maundered in barracks outside Jackson for almost a year. It was a slow torture of irony, as you can imagine: they were perhaps more safe protecting this city which no enemy (as yet) gave any thought to belaboring, than if they had stayed home to organize fire brigades among the schoolchildren. Certainly more distant from action than if they had marched with Judge Cullum to Tennessee. This may be the time, then, when Uriah began telling your grandfather about his friend Surrat, and the uncle in Nashville. Uriah may even have confided to your grandfather his raptures of choked steamy loneliness over the young bride left behind, in that feverish venereal languor which had infected him, with the onset of garrison boredom, so much more quickly than he had expected. And your grandfather sharing those symptoms, of which he knew none himself, with the man-virgin's glossy-eyed envy, credulity and adulation. Who knows what they talked about, the young bachelor and the young married orphan now soldiers waiting quietly to be shoved off to face the hot end of their first enemy rifle? Who knows? Not I, too old now to recall if I had ever known. If anyone you, assuming you are old enough yet to have found out, suspected, learned, which whether you are or not and have or have not I your father must assume you are not and have not. So I leave that to you. Suffice it they talked. Because in that general hiatus not so much false peace as period of invertible clumsy confusion which followed Manassas, there was little else they could do.

"Even their own commander had betrayed them, deserted them, they must have felt: for Buck Van Dorn was no man to endure maundering. He had resigned the Mississippi command, and was now at the head of all cavalry in Virginia.

"Van Dorn: if ever that bright gallant glomeration of courage and foolish knavery and foredestined but meaningless doom, which humankind chose to label in this particular occurrence the Confederacy, found incarnation in one man alone, it was General Earl Van Dorn. He must have been forty by then, nearly my age. Sallow, mustachioed, unmarried, he was imperious but never languid, he was devious (some say diabolical), he was quick. Quick: both on horseback (where they say he rode like a centaur but perhaps they only mean satyr) and in council and (so it appears) in the company of the fair sex. He was a man of desperate ambition. He stood five feet five: just two inches taller than Napoleon.

"Then Davis moved Van Dorn to the Transmississippi, commanding an assemblage of Indians and trappers and rangers in the West among very few settlements or roads and often through snow. Well enough, Van Dorn vowed, then he would march up the River and capture St. Louis. And this time your grandfather and Uriah were more fortunate. They succeeded in having themselves borrowed, along with the rest of a cavalry troop, by the new western commander.

"So they finally departed their home state, in early winter of '62, for the far corner of Arkansas. You can imagine their feelings during that long winter ride, I am sure: they had said goodbye to wives and mothers and boyhood now a year past, receiving nothing in balance but the dreary routine of a garrison. They had been cheated, perhaps they felt, forced to live one additional year toward the flaccid decrepitude of old age, and perhaps they swore that their eventual battle fury would be all the more heedless and furious, the hard grim conditions of wilderness war all the more welcome, for the delay. You can guess what they felt. But imminent now was the promised, the awaited: riding to action with Earl Van Dorn. Then they arrived at the Arkansas headquarters only to hear that Van Dorn was bedridden.

"And not long after that, a full Union army crossed the line into north Mississippi," *you read.*

Maybe Henry can guess what they felt. Not you. Still, maybe by now you have passed from mystification to curiosity. Maybe by now you don't need or desire to pause for relief. You might even want to know what ailed the little General.

VAN DORN, you read, had been thrown from a horse. His back, cracked or disjointed, was paining him bitterly. The aide who had followed him over the same jump, Reverend Graham relates parenthetically to Henry, and through Henry to you, had been sent back to Little Rock with a concussion. But Van Dorn's spine injury made little difference, as Uriah James and Henry's grandfather would soon discover. Riding supine in his ambulance wagon, Earl Van Dorn led the attack at Pea Ridge. Reverend Graham describes the battle.

It was Van Dorn's first debacle. Attempting a double encirclement, he was himself encircled, and in a stand at the Elkhorn Tavern lost one thousand of his men. Uriah James and Henry's grandfather escaped. What they felt, put to rout through the woods from their first engagement, their commander at fault—Reverend Graham leaves that, he says, to Henry. And of course, by transference, to you.

In March, Van Dorn was alerted by Beauregard to bring his divisions east. The Creole, says Reverend Graham, expected assault by a large Federal army outside of Corinth, Mississippi. Boxcars would be waiting at Memphis to rush Van Dorn and his men into action. So Shiloh was fought. But Van Dorn missed it. He arrived in time for the retreat. The army of Halleck took Corinth.

Next Van Dorn was left to hold Vicksburg. And now this, says Reverend Graham, would be the first view for Uriah James of those fortified bluffs. He implies that Uriah was to return. Then, in his fascination with Earl Van Dorn's campaign biography, Reverend Graham seems to forget what he has implied.

It was garrison duty again, but more strategically critical than at Jackson. Vicksburg by now, as everyone recognized, was the link holding together two halves of the Confederacy. And there was at least a token threat to be parried, from Farragut and his gunboats, assailing the unassailable cliffs. Uriah and Henry's grandfather would have spent guard time on the parapets, according to Reverend Graham. They would have looked down over the Union navy below, the Union troops on the Arkansas side of the river. They may even have worked on those entrenchments which Uriah was later to run, says Reverend Graham. Van Dorn had no difficulty holding Vicksburg. But he grew restless again for action more daring. He still wanted St. Louis. He wanted New Orleans. He wanted Memphis.

By September, he had decided to strike back at Corinth. A Union garrison remained there under Rosecrans. To Van Dorn, it seemed the linchpin of the Federals' western line. On September 24, he established his headquarters three days west of the town of Corinth. Reverend Graham stresses this point ponderously, to Henry (who wouldn't have needed any such geographical reminder) and to you (who do): three days west of Corinth, at Hadrian, Mississippi.

⁓

"So THEY were home," said Reverend Graham. "Your grandfather and Uriah. But also *not* home, of course: simply more butternut soldiers bivouacked again upon the indulgence of a peaceable town, which they viewed with a mixture of yearning and condescension and which viewed them in turn with a mixture of pride and fear, only in this case the town happened to be for those two particular troopers their own, and the imposed-upon townspeople feeling the pride and doing the fearing for cornfield and chicken coop and daughter happened to include their own parents and wife. Your grandfather returned home, for at least one Sunday dinner of which I have had account, and the same bumptious mother of one and a half years earlier needed only a single look into the face of her erstwhile boy-child to discern aright that this veteran of the Elkhorn Tavern would neither require, deserve nor tolerate any more of her maternal fussing. And so, to her credit, she spared him. He was invited formally into the office and proffered a drink from the sideboard by your great-grandfather and served a hot dinner of ham and turkey and asked polite questions about his view of the course of the campaign, and then allowed to return, in peace and dignity, as he told me, to his war. And so he was not only no longer a boy, but a man. Because the mother of his suckled infancy had said, Yes, it is true. He told me himself: it was on that day, more than any preceding or after and including that wild ragged morning of terror called the Elkhorn Tavern, on that day here in this house, he felt himself admitted to manhood. And Uriah would have returned home as well.

"Who can say what he found there. Certainly I will not say, nor can you. He returned to the young wife, the casual playfellow of his unorphaned youth by now two years a spouse and one and a half a stranger, who already knew widowhood better than her own living husband, and perhaps they tasted joy. Perhaps in this single insular moment of one day and a night or perhaps two or at most three, they tasted a sleek bitter joy more desperate and true than any that marriage had so far attained or would attain again after, and they knew it, and then it was gone. We cannot say whether they did or did not. Uriah never afterwards spoke to your grandfather of this visit, so far as I know. But let us give them that much. A moment of sad bliss, let us say. And a son was conceived, let us say. Why shouldn't we give them that much?

"Then Van Dorn marched on Corinth."

AND INTO ANOTHER DISASTER. He attacked Rosecrans in position, losing five thousand men. Reverend Graham describes it, supplying Henry and you with a blinding abundance of tactical detail.

Van Dorn was now reviled in the Confederate Senate, accused of drunkenness on duty at Corinth. Rumors spread about negligence, whoring and dissipation. A court of inquiry was called, but the rumors were discredited—at least according to Reverend Graham. Pemberton was appointed to the Mississippi command, over Van Dorn's head. Earl Van Dorn's fortunes were low. His career, though the good Reverend doesn't state it in quite these terms, was in the toilet.

In December the reversal began. Again the little General was leading cavalry. Pemberton sent him out to skirt Grant, camped at Oxford, and to threaten his lines of supply. The Federal storebase was Hadrian. Reverend Graham's voice rises here to a whisper. At dawn on December 20, he says, Van Dorn thundered suddenly back into the town.

⁓

"AND NOW LISTEN," said Reverend Graham. "Listen with your memory and your blood and hold your heart up a beat and you will see it, you will be there, hearing the sharp hollow hoofbeats of a cavalry charge over frozen mud, the mud of the very road before which you now sit, like the roar of a waterfall approached gradually and then glimpsed. They came on at a full gallop. Listen now and you may hear it, just as I who was unborn yet myself have heard it, more than once, in the silence and the earth which is still the same piece of earth and in my own blood, which is also the same. Listen with your blood," Reverend Graham said. Henry listened.

"So Van Dorn captured the garrison, and paroled them, and put the torch to a one-million-dollar depot of Grant's food and equipment. And thus set a whole Yankee army into retreat. Your grandfather had never expected that burning his own town could be so glorious. The depot was south of the square but the flames climbed like a mountain against the dull flat December sky and your great-grandparents watched it from this gallery. Your great-grandfather called for a pitcher of toddies, I am told, and toasted the spectacle on behalf of Earl Van Dorn and his own son, who had supplied the spark, and U. S. Grant, who had supplied the fuel. Perhaps Grant himself watched it from Oxford, or smelled it, or felt that cold silent murmur of black intuition in his soldier's bones. Then they turned in the saddle and rode out for Tennessee.

"And whether Uriah was able to stop home again here on the day of the raid, I do not know. He may have. Your grandfather did not. But Uriah may have. And if he did, perhaps it was now that he noted a change, a gentle disquieting transformation in the attitude of the young wife, who (so it seems) was no longer the same devoted stranger with whom he had known the September bliss. He may have detected the change then, if the change by then had occurred. Or he may not. And he rode with the others for Tennessee.

"Then in March it was Thompson's Station. Van Dorn was riding skirmish for Bragg now, over the desperate protests of Pemberton, who wanted him also, and suddenly there weren't enough Earl Van Dorns to satisfy one Confederacy. Thompson's Station, and this time in concert with Forrest, against a full infantry column. They sent prisoners and artillery south while Van Dorn went after more Yankees. His blood was up like a coon dog's in a cross-country chase. He slashed back and forth throughout that part of Tennessee, playing hell on Rosecrans's lines. Next a garrisoned railroad bridge at the Little Harpeth River: more prisoners, more supplies, more vindication.

"Fortune's smile was upon him again, as Van Dorn himself would have sensed, believing not in the arrival of good luck but in the final departure of the bad, so that native cunning and daring and sureness at last disencumbered could redeem his deserved reputation. He did not begin to feel satisfaction, of course. Buck Van Dorn had not set out in this war to achieve mere redemption, vindication, after having been marked down in succession an incompetent, a coward and (not unlike Grant) an irresponsible drunk. No, success would have only heightened his thirst for that draught of glory he had sampled in Hadrian. The general order for the month would commend his brilliance in two separate affairs. Van Dorn would not linger to savor it. He was moving toward Franklin. He was thinking, it is easy enough to imagine, of Nashville.

"And then the 7th of May. He was headquartered at Spring Hill, Tennessee. On that morning he sat alone in his tent, bent over the camp desk, at work. He was concocting more plans of harassment, we can assume, his brain now afever with blood and hoofclatter and glory. The man's name was Peters, a local physician. But whether traitor or paid assassin or simply outraged cuckold husband to a willing young patriot, we cannot say. Husband they claim, and Van Dorn was a man made of what all men are, so perhaps we must take their word. But we do not know. He entered the tent unnoticed, this Dr. Peters, and put his pistol to the back of Van Dorn's head and fired, and then rode off again in his buggy. By the time he safely passed Union lines, Earl Van Dorn was dead."

III

"BUT IF IT WAS Surrat himself who called off the wedding,"

said Henry, "why didn't she and the son just elope? Or why didn't Miss Louisa go after Cham, when he left?"

"Ah," Reverend Graham said again. "She was from Illinois, yes. But they had made her a Southern lady, you recall: she had learned how to wait.

"It would have been 1884 when the town had its first look at her. She was a girl of eighteen then, pale and erect and almost as tall as a man of moderate height, with thin features not yet drawn to gauntness and her own claim, so they say, to a certain tenuous cool beauty. She moved with bearing, if not grace, her chin held carefully high as though to assert an embattled pride or to balance a saucer atop her head, but her dark eyes belied that gesture of steadiness. Her eyelids were tremulous, fluttering ever on the verge of a pained squint, as though against wind-driven dust. She said little in company, during that visit. The town did not get to know her. She seemed shy, and frightened, and anxious to please—which she did not do, particularly. It was Christmas, and she had come over from Oxford, for a holiday near him who was later to be her intended. Oh yes, she was beautiful in her way, they might have conceded; but she seemed to them weightless, lacking solidity, like the swamp-risen butterfly of one day's fleeting existence sent into the sky without ballast of stomach and gut and all the heavy organs of experience. The dust storm when it came, they believed, would sweep this creature away.

"She had been sent South the year previous, from Illinois. She was enrolled by her family, whoever they were, in the Women's Academy at Oxford. What purblind rustic innocence may have merited anyone in the belief that she would find something at that institution worth the journey, we will never know. She arrived on the train one September morning, they say, wearing the gray heavy dress and traveling bonnet that may have been stylish or comfortable enough in Illinois and bearing only a single wickerwork suitcase, an empty hamper that had held fruit for the ride, and a look of such waifish bewilderment that the stationmaster must have wondered whether she hadn't made the wrong switch of trains in St. Louis. 'Is this Mississippi?' she asked in her pruning-saw Illinois voice. 'Is this Oxford, Mississippi?' To her eternal misfortune, it was.

"Whether she regained some of her home-bred poise, if there was any, with what acceptance and friendship she may have been vouchsafed among the other young girls and the duennas of the Academy that year, or whether it was to the Academy itself that she owed the saucer-carrying trick, is hard to say. The year was not unmitigated wormwood, apparently (though I cannot believe she found it easy) because she remained. There may have been friends, or at least a single particular friend, a confidante; there must have been, for she remained. There would have been social evenings, parties, the usual ruthlessly chaperoned Harvest and Christmas and Mardi Gras balls with the young men from the University, and at some of these she would have made acquaintances and filled a part of her card and danced. She was never a belle. For all her beauty, for all her carriage, for all her efforts if she made efforts, she never lost that rigid intent air of foreignness, that stern (you'll excuse my pun) opacity, which left her formidable to all but the few. She was different, and she could not herself say why, and she for that reason seemed to carry a burden of mysteriousness. In some women this would have been exotic, irresistible. In Louisa Sterne, apparently, it was not.

"Yet she remained, not even returning to Illinois that summer but staying on at Oxford as guest or companion or perhaps housegirl to one of the duennas. She did not stay because of her fondness for Oxford, we can presume, nor out of love, since so far as we know she had not yet at that time met Chamberlain Surrat. She stayed through the summer because her people could not afford another train ticket so soon, she may have explained. Or because her father was traveling (and her mother long dead), she may have explained. In truth, she already had little home to which to return, I suspect. You can't help but sense it in the earlier joyless arrival: that whatever conditions in Illinois had precipitated her exile to north Mississippi, she would not be required back for a summer.

"She met him that autumn. We do not know the occasion. Whether at a ball or in a casual encounter through one of their friends or whether he had viewed her afar now for months with increasing avidity and finally bolstered himself to speak to her, only she or Cham Surrat could tell us, and she surely would not. So the first appearance of Miss Louisa by word or flesh to reach Hadrian would have come in the letter of early December that Cham wrote to his father: a young lady would be visiting over Christmas. Homeless still, she had accepted the invitation from a female acquaintance to see Hadrian for the holidays. Of course this was a ploy, an obliging complicitous machination by the classmate through which Miss Louisa could in all propriety and discretion be near the young man of her interest. Cham wrote his father, preparing the way for their own bachelor hospitality toward the young lady, and perhaps he mentioned her name.

"Yes, that's right: actually wrote of it to his father. Oh, I know what you say, I know the very idea sounds to you strange, archaic, perhaps this more than anything setting the whole lot of them beyond pale of credible human experience and into the realm of stereopticon slide or wedding-cake figurines, or farther, history: that a man would confide the first flight of his youthful heart to, of all people, his father. Believe me I know.

"Yet that much is true: it not only may be, it must be. Cham wrote ahead, disclosing his feelings, or at least his intentions (strictly honorable, as we know) to his father. And he could do that, it was possible. Because their relationship was unique (as even the town had noted and viewed with puzzled deference since Chamberlain's boyhood), quite unlike the usual tortuous mutual bloodletting entanglement of father and son. They were two gentlemen, who found congenial the arrangement of sharing not only lodgings but a name. Or so it seemed.

"Because Cham was his own creature, headstrong and parentless as a mule. He stood removed from his father by a gulf not of hostility nor rebellion but merely indifference, self-sufficiency, freed of the need to struggle for freedom in a way that boys of his age seldom achieve and some grown men never. The town hadn't noticed just when it happened. Some indeterminate moment of boyhood, perhaps when the mother was torn away, perhaps when Cham spent his first autumn night rain-drenched in hunting camp, or shot his first deer or beat his first nigger (or perhaps he had been brought to cold abrupt manhood by a high-yellow servant girl in the haybarn), had triggered the change, but the town only grasped it gradually, after the fact, and remained divided in their opinions as to the cause. Whether Surrat himself, the father, had been more sensitive to the event, or at least more prompt in his adjustment to the consequences, we do not know. Probably he was. There is no recollection of father and son having passed through a period of conflict. They must have mutually acceded to the new arrangement as quickly as either sensed its arrival. After all, Surrat had the negative example of the Nashville uncle to aid him in this. And no man in the town had ever faulted Joseph Surrat as short of memory or heedless of precedent.

"Cham had laid full claim to this independence by the age of fourteen or fifteen; and Surrat, a busy man with his own affairs, was evidently amenable. Neither command nor obedience, nor what could be called love, passed between them: only a certain comradely respect, and information. So you can imagine the letter. No one but Surrat, of course, ever saw it.

"Still, I doubt that even Chamberlain Surrat would have said more than 'a young lady from the Academy here.' More than 'a young lady from the Academy, of whom I am privileged to have the acquaintance, and who as it happens will be visiting in Hadrian over Christmas.' Perhaps he did. Perhaps he said that her name was Louisa, or even Louisa Sterne, that she was a Yankee girl from Illinois but very agreeable nonetheless, and perhaps he even allowed himself to speak of the sharp features, the sober carriage, the shadowy, almost hooded, gray eyes, the dark bundle of hair. I doubt it. I prefer to believe he would have spoken only of 'a young lady,' not from embarrassment but in the upright formality which he and Surrat observed, much as Rembrandt might have titled a sensitive portrait, 'Young lady in a wool coat.' So we must assume that the day of that fastidious afternoon tea at the bachelor household in Hadrian was the first occasion on which Joseph Surrat could have suspected that his future presumptive daughter-in-law was not only a Northerner but a Jew."

It was dark now, dark enough almost to suit Miss Louisa, Henry guessed, at least considering the additional half-light he would expend in bringing the phaeton around and driving the mile or more across the square to her house not to mention the two miles farther out the Jackson road to the Old Governor's house, first crossing the square once again (this partly at least why she required darkness, he understood: the square-crossing) though not yet dark enough it seemed for his father. Reverend Graham's voice did not cease. It merely paused, suspending itself breathless and unfinal in the moment's timeless distraction of refilling the bowl of his pipe. Fireflies were gathering in the umbrageous void below them that not long before had held the languid cream blossoms of magnolia and the cedars in neat rows, now dissolved within waning twilight, and opposite his own chair amid watery shadows Henry observed the quick minnow-like flash of the small tool accepting its share of the dying light. Henry thought of Miss Louisa. He saw her waiting for him in the dim airless front room of her one-story cottage, the house itself squat in the night like a small pumpkin carved to a grim misanthropic Halloween scowl by someone with a talent for grimness, except that even now the house's windows and door would not glow yellow. She would be waiting for him in the dark, Henry guessed. Perhaps because she would be leaving the house soon and an acquaintance had once told her that the cost of electricity was measured not in the actual time the light burned but by the successive cumulative thrusts taken to overcome primary inertia when the switch was snapped; or because she was already adjusting her eyes to the night. Perhaps she was in fact that keen and that desperate. He pictured her, in the dark room, seated less now like his father's Rembrandt than like a Whistler, with bonnet and shawl and her hands folded carefully onto her lap in patient stillness that was yet somehow furious; waiting. He thought back to his father's words. She has learned how, Henry thought. She has waited these twenty-eight years. I guess she can wait an hour longer, he thought. Then the smell of tobacco bloomed again like a night flower and Reverend Graham raised his feet back to the railing.

"Because Surrat misjudged his own son, just as Chamberlain had misjudged his father," Reverend Graham said. "It was the gentlemen's agreement that foiled them, I believe, the false assumption that they could ever be anything but predaceously interbound to each other's lives. He who had set Chamberlain's utter freedom above his own paternal compulsions and set untiring service to his community above both now seemed to set, before all, the hungry dogs of his own ambition, driving willfully from his life the very son of his widower's flagging years who might have been judged his main compensation for accepting and serving in the position to which he aspired. So he would find it ash to his tongue. But Chamberlain would not be around to take pleasure in that.

"They returned the next year, Cham and the young woman, at Christmas of '85, with word this time preceding them not only to Surrat but along the channels established and tended for such gossip throughout the whole town, because this time the word was *fiancée*. The news must have come first from Cham himself, or from the female acquaintance whose home was in Hadrian (it cannot have come from Miss Louisa, who was still to everyone here a complete stranger): an engagement to be announced over the holidays. Chamberlain Surrat would marry Miss Louisa Sterne, of Rock Island, Illinois. Of course, his father had already heard of it, been informed, with courteous matter-of-factness though without any application for parental approval, in one of the letters. So Surrat was not circumvented, nor caught by surprise. This was just at the juncture when forces favorable to his candidacy had begun to come into promising alignment but long before any open campaigning, and he would have had time to think. He bided that time. As far as we know Surrat had given Chamberlain, the Christmas before, no reason to suspect that he had any objections personal or otherwise to this particular young lady. But that is only as far as we know. Then it was Christmas. And suddenly with no warning like the thunderclap over an unwary May picnic, this: he asked Miss Louisa to excuse himself and his son, and invited Chamberlain into the library.

"So something happened. Nobody in town knew what: a discussion, a confession of some sort by the son or a revelation of some sort by the father or at least a new factor introduced into the balance, and an argument, whether between father and son or between Chamberlain and his fiancée, nobody knew. At least nobody knew until word got around town that Surrat had forbidden the marriage, and that Chamberlain had this time of all times accepted his father's fiat. But whatever, when Christmas day came, Chamberlain Surrat was gone.

"Miss Louisa remained. Oh, she fled from that bachelor household on a crest of speechless humiliation, of course, fled all the way back to Oxford and the hard sexless safety of cold pressed linen and Minervan virginity in the dormitory of the Women's Academy. The town believed for as long as two weeks that she had followed Cham, lit out to join him in Memphis or Jackson where by hastily arranged rendezvous they were meeting to consummate not only the love but the defiance. And the town pretended to be horrified. Then the vacation was over and the female acquaintance returned to send back from Oxford news at which the town was genuinely horrified: Miss Louisa was still there. Silent and livid and implacable, the fine erect features already wilted like orchids before flame to a pallid caricature of what they had been, she seemed to be waiting.

"She remained at the Academy six months. Then, confounding the town's expectations still further, she betook herself back here to Hadrian. She apparently had a few pennies by then saved or inherited. She found a room in a respectable house and got permission to put out a sign for lessons in china-painting and piano. And again, she seemed to be waiting. Needless to say, the good ladies of town were more horrified than ever. Out of pure embarrassment for her, I believe, they began sending their own daughters as fast as the little girls could be dressed and pushed out the door, for the piano and the china-painting. Such a yawning breach in propriety or pride or whatever it was had to be filled somehow, you see, quickly, at once, and this was the first way they seized on of doing it. So she had the best of them after all, of the whole town, who have now supplied her a steady if pitiful living these twenty-eight years in remittance only for the outrage she suffered and would not let them forget and the two meager skills that were all the Women's Academy had managed to teach her.

"What she thought of it, whether she knew or understood or accepted the reason for Chamberlain Surrat's desertion or suspected where he had gone, what she hoped for or expected, why she stayed: the town never learned any of this. She did not volunteer her secrets, and no one in even twenty-eight years, I am sure, has had the brashness to face her and ask. She was waiting, and knew how, and that was enough for them, finally.

"But why you, of all people in this town and its history, why you to whom the lifetime of deafening silence should be broken (save that you have a name she perhaps feels she can count upon if not fully trust and a rig to take her where she feels she needs to be taken and two hands to do whatever may be expected of you when you get there) is one of those abiding and beautifully seamless mysteries confined to the bulb of an onion and the far reach of the universe and the mind of the Southern woman." Now it was Reverend Graham who waited.

"Nossir," Henry answered. "She hasn't said."

"So Surrat went down to Jackson, duly elected as the un-Reconstructed Bourbon who had stood with Beauregard and

Robert Lee, and unencumbered by any daughters-in-law of woodpile lineage. Nor by any family of his own now, whatever. At sixty, he was alone, as he had been at the start. He did not make a bad Governor, nor an especially good one. He simply served, doing his time as the uncautious bankteller caught in a moment of weakness after hours with his hand in the Wells-Fargo box does his time, patiently, with quiet regretful forbearance, and some bitterness. Oh, Surrat began with flair, a show of energy and fresh resoluteness and a summer heat storm of rhetoric. That was the stage at which he asked your grandfather to join the administration. Then he ran into problems, just the usual inert petty problems of greed and sloth and contrariety inherent in governing any state full of Mississippians, as he should have and indeed must have foreseen. But with that, or for some other reason, the energy seemed to fade. This much I myself can remember: toward the end of that term in office, his first and his only, he had already come to be known, at least among those of us here in Hadrian, as the *Old* Governor. Then he quit. One term was enough, or more than enough. And he came home.

"He was an unhappy man. Even you must recall how he looked, on those weekly occasions when he would hobble forbiddingly uptown to the square for the mail which the postmaster usually did not have for him or the cigars which appeared to give him so little pleasure: as though rehearsing over and over in his mind, like the bankteller at yard exercise, how the grim perversity of events had betrayed him.

"So the town saw or heard little of Joe Surrat during the last decade and a half of his life, and this family less than the rest of the town. Because he still carried his bitterness, you see, over your grandfather's rejection. Oh yes, he must have been furious at the time and neither man ever forgot it. Surrat had offered to bring your grandfather down to Jackson as commissioner of all Mississippi railroads and set him into an office with a staff of footmen to work for him, and your grandfather had said, Not on his life. The exact terms into which he cast that refusal even I do not know, and I believe only the two of them, stubborn and laconic men both, ever did. Your grandfather did not like to talk of it. He declined to tell me why he had spurned the job (though I saw that he would have refused to share in any enterprise of which Joseph Surrat was author, be it running the state or saving a county poorbox from high water) and if even your grandmother knew the reason it was by osmosis and intuition. He simply did not approve of the man, Surrat. He never said why. But I suspected until the day of his death, and do still, that it was the marriage. The marriage that had produced (or at least, to which was born) Chamberlain Surrat was in your grandfather's mind a public abomination, I think. Because your grandfather believed (despite verified evidence to the contrary) that Uriah James was alive. But he wouldn't say why.

"I still have the letters he wrote to your great-grandmother. I have read every letter. (Just as you should; perhaps I will bring them down from the attic before you go North.) Three of them are dated from Johnston's camp outside Jackson, in those dark anxious days that followed the death of Van Dorn, when the War was lost, not by carnage or stupidity (as some say) but by caution. So I know something of what he thought, and what he saw, though he never afterward spoke of it. It is there on the yellowing pages, some of them by now broken in half at the crease, and scrawled down in a young soldier's hurried hand, perhaps with stove polish dipped up on a sharp hollow reed, to his 'Dearest Mother'. And what is not there, can be imagined.

"Leaderless after that day in Spring Hill, Uriah and your grandfather were sent with their company to provide eyes for Joe Johnston, whose relief expedition was assembling at Jackson. They rode direct and arrived before Old Joe, who came roundabout on the train. By that time Sherman had gotten his corps turned around from helping drive Pemberton back into Vicksburg, and was threatening the very capital where Johnston was expected. Johnston no sooner appeared and spent one night in the city than he had to retreat, letting Sherman put torch to the statehouse. But not before Johnston had sent off a message to Pemberton. Old Joe himself held only one division then, and to his mind it was Pemberton who should do the relieving. As a precaution, Johnston sent the identical dispatch by three different volunteer couriers. It said: 'Sherman is between us at Clinton. Come up in his rear at once.' And one of those three volunteers was Uriah James.

"So Uriah ran the siege, two days alone in the saddle with only a few minutes of rest and no sleep dodging Yankee outriders and pickets in the woods east of Vicksburg, and was the first of the three to deliver Johnston's message to Pemberton. At least that's what your grandfather believed. But his view was not the only one. Because on the night of the day Johnston retreated before Sherman, Grant himself was in Jackson, in the very hotel room where Old Joe had stayed the night previous, receiving a copy of Johnston's dispatch. It had been betrayed to him by one of the three couriers.

"With that useful knowledge, revealing Johnston's passivity, Grant was safe to turn round and finish the job of bottling Pemberton up inside Vicksburg. He and Sherman sat down at the gates, while Joe Johnston remained off by himself to the northeast, stewing in camp with a fresh force he considered too small for even attempting relief. And at the end of the week, Joseph Surrat arrived from Virginia, transferred to Johnston's staff.

"I cannot tell you, of course, what they felt, Uriah and Surrat, meeting again here in the lengthening shadows of a lost war. Perhaps there was great distance, bitterness, even hatred, between the two former friends. It is easy enough to imagine that. Surrat in less than three months was to take the younger man's wife for his own. Perhaps the liaison itself, and at least its covetous premeditation, had already taken form. If Uriah sensed this, he faced Surrat with a murderous cold eye.

"But I suspect it was otherwise. In that brief visit home at the time of Van Dorn's raid, Uriah cannot have learned much. If he perceived that a sickening reversal had robbed him of the young wife's affections, she would not have admitted the name of his rival. He certainly could not have guessed. And he did not linger long enough for gossip from town to reach him. So whatever Joseph Surrat may have known of their altered relations, surely Uriah knew less. In fact, I believe he would have viewed Surrat, now a staff officer at the headquarters from which he served, with much the same boyish adulation that he had contracted for this man at the age of nine.

"Perhaps he even felt pride. Perhaps he was anxious to prove before Surrat his own manly daring. Perhaps that was the reason he continued to volunteer.

"Uriah made four rides in all, bearing Johnston's dispatches to Pemberton. Three times, by reckless and superior horsemanship (according to your grandfather), he passed the Yankee lines. On the fourth, they sent him with two men for an escort. So he was killed.

"The body was found in a bayou. And news came back to Hadrian that Uriah had died in the act of treason.

"This was late June," said Reverend Graham. "Into the fortieth day of the siege. Inside Vicksburg, Pemberton was still holding his walls and feeding his soldiers and townspeople on the last of the bacon and the first of the mules and the grainy moist bread they were making from ground peas, and living with them in dirt caves under the deadly incessant shelling. Johnston, outside, was still making excuses: he was awaiting another division, he was awaiting more guns or more wagons, he was waiting for Pemberton himself to initiate a breach that would draw Grant out of position. Richmond was screaming across the wires for Johnston to move, to do something, anything, for if Vicksburg and the River and the Transmississippi were lost, then the Cause itself was surely lost too. But Johnston delayed, more concerned for the safety and readiness of his army, which by his own estimation was too slight for a critical undertaking, than for the defense of any single fixed point, however strategic. Meanwhile Pemberton's men, swollen at the ankles with scurvy and feverish with starvation and half of their number already on sick list or in the hospital, could look down over their works just a few yards to see the Federal trenches and mines gnawing inexorably up the hillside toward the very doomed earth under their own feet.

"Then it was over. Johnston finally moved. Cautiously, behind cavalry, he advanced toward Grant's rearward line. He arrived within earshot on the Fourth of July. Of course, he was too late. Joe Johnston stood on a hill in the woods and pricked up his ears toward the city, but this day of all days the mortars and cannon were silent.

"Because just that morning, the garrison had marched out in an ordered column, to pile their weapons quietly on the grass. And Grant had ridden with Pemberton to the courthouse," said Reverend Graham. Bringing his feet down from the railing, he began to grope in the dark for a match.

Yes, Henry thought, now I have heard it too many times. *But maybe you haven't.*

IV

"SO THEY WILL have told you doubtless already," Miss Louisa said, "how I reneged at the last on that outrage and pride and bitterness which alone had supplied form (you will notice I do not presume to say meaning) to my life those twenty-three years, and rode out there to nurse Surrat's final illness. They will have told you about it, how in response to some more or less brusque or abject (they could not decide about this, unsure as they were whether he or myself was the more stubborn, the more confirmed in our rigid implacable solipsism, the less likely to budge before threat, promise, or pacification and unfathoming how either of us could ever be either persuadable or persuasive) summons or perhaps only in answer to a quaint perverse inner daimon of my own, I mounted the box of that buggy beside the middle-aged nigger man he still called his boy, and as a graying and stinted old woman traversed these two miles to the household I had last seen as a thwarted bride. They will have told you that much; or perhaps you have a memory of it yourself. It is not so very long ago now, only five years, and that nothing to a lifetime, even an empty one. Perhaps you, a child then at play in the dirt, may have chanced to look up and note the incongruous couple, the white dowager-maiden and the nigger man-boy, riding out this very road speechless, undivertible and as though frozen in sudden upright catalepsis, through the dust of a June afternoon, toward their destination. Yes, I went in the full heat of day then, having nothing to hide.

"Oh, I do not claim that either he or myself, Joseph Surrat or myself, we two atrophic husks of what had formerly been persons, could at that time have been the object of much active curiosity, even among a small townful of narrow and under-occupied Methodists. No, you must not mistake me about that. But I went by full daylight, through the square as we do now, and someone or other will have noticed, and from them you too will have heard, when the lugubrious little subject of our two lugubrious little lives found its turn. Yet they will not have said why.

"They cannot have told you why, because they do not know. They cannot have told you how it took not one summons (brought by hand of the same portly dull Hermes, the nigger man apparently middle-aged but ageless behind his inscrutable mocha expression of servile indifference and boredom and languor, the short nappy whorls of hair flecked as with a sprinkling of white sugar and the whole globular body ridiculous in its cast-down waistcoat and vest and gold watch chain without I suspect any watch on its pocket-end like a penumbrous Stygian proxy of Surrat himself, the rolls and folds of perspiring indolent mocha flesh giving the aspect of a great soft Buddha in chocolate or amber candlewax nearing the critical temperature at which it would melt down to warm liquid inside the hot clothes and be gone; carried to town the previous day and rejected for its miscast presumption with quick acrid disdain and as summarily as the second summons, a day later, would be accepted) but two before I would mount up to the box beside the sweating nigger and ride out there to face him again. Isn't that right?"

"Yessum," Henry said.

"It was because we had nothing to say to each other," Miss Louisa declared. "Nothing in all God's benighted world. Joseph Surrat and I were more than just strangers or enemies, you see: we were the consummation of both—both blood-foes in that most barbaric and gore-thirsty of human embattlements, the family feud, and also cold stark strangers—who had lived for two decades together apart in devouring reaffirmation of that relationship. So when the second message arrived, explaining that he had something to tell me before he died, I of course went. I knew it must if nothing else be the truth. Because when two strangers meet who have naught to expect from each other, naught to offer each other, there is no longer reason for lies. And perhaps that also is something you will have learned for yourself today."

"Yessum," he said.

"I went out there. I sent the nigger and the other servants away, and I waited for the bald outrageous words I had been led to believe I would hear. But of course, I had only been fooled again. Cunning?—yes he was cunning, more cunning than they knew, more cunning than anyone save myself and Uriah and perhaps Chamberlain ever had cause to suspect. He would not speak. He would not say his piece. He was not yet convinced (so he claimed) that he was indeed going to die. And he did not want to be premature.

"I might have killed him myself at that moment. Surrat had summoned me, I had come, because in his harrowing guilt he dreaded to carry the secret alone to his grave. But neither did he want to reveal it to me, and live. So we waited. I nursed him without mercy or pity and he lingered without hope or concern. Then he took a turn, and knew it; but I sent for the doctor nevertheless, marching the man afterward back into the death chamber to pronounce for those very Faustian ears the Mephistophelian foreclosure: Surrat could not live out the night. And so it was, late that afternoon, he told me what he had told Chamberlain, confessing the neat bloodless aseptic lie he had used in destroying my life.

"I will not judge him. I leave that to others of you, the on-lookers and descendants of onlookers and phagocytes of historical alimentation who come afterward owning distance and leisure enough for such luxuries. I have neither. I possess only the facts. That is the final testament of my poverty.

"Surrat had returned to the town in October of '62, you see, having arranged some sort of furlough, perhaps claiming a month to stop home from Virginia and bring in his crop. He had no crop. No crop in the ground, at least, neither cotton nor cane nor corn, no product of his own honest sweat nor that of his slaves, none that had already been planted before his return. (The only crop he was to gather from this visit would ripen later, much later, those nine months or twenty-three years that saw the sweet-bitter mammalian garden-fruit come to term and burst with the fullness to scatter its spore like a sirocco-born virulence on the dry winds of love and ambition and time.) His bachelor cabin in town was never opened. He did not appear on the square. Most of the good people of Hadrian were unaware of his presence. Even I cannot tell you just how long he was here. But the facts, laconic and unerring, speak in my place: Colonel Surrat's horse was seen taking oats in the barn of the James homestead, on the outskirts of town.

"During what space of loveless nights he had cowled the flame of adulterous greed for Uriah's young wife, I do not know. At most (we may assume) two years, from the last days of darkening peace, since before that Ruth James was no more than a schoolgirl, and set beyond reach of Surrat's leer perhaps not by age nor experience nor decency and certainly not civic propriety but simply the thirty short miles that separated Oxford from Hadrian and her girlhood from his bachelordom. (Besides, what could have caused him to notice her, she who was quiet and comely but not beautiful, no more alluring than any one of the drove of unmarried daughters he had ignored in the last dozen years, and not yet another man's wife?) But while under apprenticeship in his friend's law office, Uriah had rediscovered a woman in the forgotten hoyden of his childhood's halcyon summers, and married her, as though seizing by that act some familiar receptacle in which to catch and retain the ebbing lifeblood of memories and identity that his mother's death had threatened to hemorrhage forever from him, introducing this new young bride at the same time to the reptilian attention of Joseph Surrat. I doubt that Surrat had ever known love before. In fact, I doubt he did then. It must have been something else, though if we name it desire or lust even these words partake of a guileless directness unworthy of him. Suffice it that Surrat had after years of delay found something to want, to want for reasons perhaps even he did not understand, and small bother that what he found happened already to belong to his friend. When he skirted the town that October and brought his horse up to the front gallery of the James boardinghouse, of course, he had only come inquiring after Uriah.

"What moved her I cannot say, I cannot even guess, nor does it concern me. Perhaps she had never really cared for Uriah, perhaps in that gay lambent butterfly renegadery of some girls her age and station she had cared neither for him nor for anyone, anything, had married not Uriah James but his house or his future or to escape her own father or be freed formally and for all to know from the weighty hermetic carceration of her virginity, or perhaps only to see the daguerreotype of herself in the dress. Or perhaps she had indeed married him in a perfect light froth of young love, like meringue, only to find the actual living and sharing and waking and washing, and who knows but even the coupling, quite other than what she had expected, bargained for, and so in her betrayal thought only to renounce and revoke by casual fiat a disagreeable circumstance into which she felt herself betrayed. Or perhaps she simply grew tired of waiting. It had been almost a year and a half. What moved her I am not able to say, not qualified, who have waited now half a lifetime and am still waiting, however tired. And so I will not judge her. I will leave that to others, who may better understand.

"She took Surrat in. The horse which a nigger hand later identified as Colonel Surrat's was stabled in Uriah's barn for a week, or three days, or some say overnight. The time does not matter. Surrat had a furlough that month (I know this, because I have made inquiries); he was not seen on the square, nor did he open his own house; his horse was observed. Then he rode back to his war. I offer you no judgments. I do not say he conceived in adultery on the twenty-year-old body of his foster son's wife. No one will ever know that, because we have only his word. He is dead, and she is long dead and that young body rotted to humus, and Uriah too has died long ago, but facts are like stones, and do not die. Here is a fact. In July of the next year, Cham was born.

"By then Uriah was gone: the man who had married the girl who had mothered the child who would bear another man's name, was himself numbered dead, and even his mortal meat left unquiet, scavenged to the bone by hungry crawfish in a warm Delta bayou. Or so it was reported. And worse: they called him traitor.

"But traitor to what?—to a wife who had already consummated the pact of her own treachery, or to a cause already doomed from the first cannonade at Sumter and lingering stupid and bold and rapacious as a spring-woken bear in the sole capacity of providing occasion for fools and boys to die honorably and honorless blackguards to live gloriously, or to a butternut uniform, to a line of command, finally after all to a single man in position to issue a summary order neither honorable nor legitimate nor even military but as duplicitous as it was homicidal? Who indeed did Uriah betray?—who alone did this simple man surpass far enough in guile to delude and manipulate, to cashier for his own selfish ends, yes (mind you that I do not absolve him) to betray? Certainly, it was not who they thought.

"Surrat arrived west at Vicksburg again near the end of May. Coming late to this scene of the grand climacteric, he took up the cue perfectly, his timing was faultless (though some would doubt it later that summer when he married the woman who changed widow's veil for wedding lace with the ease of a mockingbird changing calls), for Uriah had been in the Johnston camp a week or more then, and had already made his first ride through the siege-lines around the city. So probably it is too much to believe (I do not deny having tried) even of Joseph Surrat, that the man arranged his own transfer from Lee to Johnston, from the right hand of honor's apotheosis to the timorous nightwatch of infamy, with murder premeditated. No, we will give him some benefit, we will allow that he was dispatched, willing or nilling, a native Mississippian (or such was their misinformation) who might prove (so they apparently thought; perhaps out in Virginia there was not the supply of distractions, diversions, other men's wives, that our soldiers were burdened with here in Mississippi and Tennessee) of particular usefulness to Johnston's mission, and discovered himself if not face to face at least sharing a headquarters camp and a commanding officer with his protégé, friend, now rival, in a singular situation whose implications he was not slow to recognize.

"As Johnston's adjutant (and my inquiries have confirmed it) Surrat bore responsibility for communications. His chore it was to call for, and to select, from among an army's small inevitable van of self-immolative zealotry and vainglory, those young volunteer couriers who would risk the bullet between their shoulderblades bearing Johnston's procrastinatory ditherings to Pemberton. And so again Uriah rode to Vicksburg. He rode four times in all, until Joseph Surrat could be sure he was dead. It was not difficult to contrive: Uriah perhaps the best horseman in his regiment and knowing the Vicksburg emplacements by now as well as anyone, and still all unawares of that new bond of enmity between himself and the man he had known as a second father. Let it be me, he told Surrat, his friend; and it was. On that final attempt to breach the investiture, Uriah James met his bullet. But it did not come between the shoulderblades, nor from a Yankee rifle.

"Yes, they called it treason, with that epic compoundment of inversion and slander and sinister genius fabrication that rose up to enrobe Uriah's supposed crime, his supposed execution, and that stands as verdict today, a monument to the susceptibility of small minds and history's indifference to truth and the cunning of Colonel Joe Surrat, C.S.A. Because not only facts are like stones: there are lies too which prevail.

"Three times, successfully, Uriah had broken through or around or over the top of Grant's siege, to enter the city of Vicksburg; alone. The peril of life, which most soldiers at least as sane as they were brave would have and indeed had declined to accept once, was not enough even three times to accomplish that end for which (no man can deny) Surrat had reason to wish. He summoned Uriah, extracted consent from (you appreciate it is only with irony that I persist in calling him) his volunteer, concocted a further mission, a fourth dispatch (although little more than a week now before Vicksburg's collapse, with Pemberton hoping but not expecting and Johnston regretting but not relenting and Joseph Surrat neither regretting nor hoping, the futility palpable and defeat looming vagrant and ineluctable as the broad callous heat of July, coming, whatever, coming) which was not and never intended to be a message for Vicksburg the doomed city but rather for

Uriah himself the doomed man, his own warrant of death and burial order and epitaph that he carried, unopened, written and sealed by Surrat's hand, and which (or such was Surrat's intent) Uriah was never to read, never to see, never to survive. And this time an escort, a pair of armed men to accompany him through the two breathless days of hedgerows and blind thickets and streambeds and the two sleepless nights, for protection, added security, Surrat would have explained (neglecting to specify whose): a corporal and a private. Joseph Surrat was never the man, as I believe I have shown you before this, to leave an affair to the whim of chance.

"You ask how I judge him, how I a mere outsider woman embittered derelict spinster not even born in the country nor yet at the time about which I speak, how I look into the heart of even a man who has so injured me in my turn, to read murder; asking not how I know but rather why I believe that I may know, and can, and must; rightfully you ask. But you are mistaken. I do not judge. I have no need for that: these are facts. An escort of two men was sent with Uriah, superintendents to his death, proxies to his executioner. And one of the two was a Private Sterne."

"We're here," Henry said. "Excuse me. Shall I turn up the drive?"

"No," she said, rasped, like a curse, "wait. Stop just where you are and wait.

"So I in my turn agreed I would marry the son, the issue, the heir if not of the same slow reptilian cunning and (some would say; I do not say) the guilt then at least of the blood and the memory and if not that then at least of the name. It was Christmas of '85 and I had come to this town for the announcement of my engagement. Soon, sooner than I could have suspected and forewarned myself of it because it was already ordained and decreed before ever existed my tenuous

brittle dreams, soon I had no engagement to announce, because (as I was informed: no, I was not the last to know,
merely the third) I had no marriage toward which I was en-
gaged; and then, soon again (too soon for a girl herself born
into a marriage that never knew love but only convenience
and necessity and raised by the widower to that marriage in
a home without love but only the minute watchful purpose-
fulness of a wraith and sent off to be educated in that
starched Southern convent to the great god Gentility lacking
not only men and knowledge of them but also freedom from
the fearful yearning anticipation of inavertible maid-servant-
hood to the hard masculine unknown, who thus at the first
touch of love had not simply fallen in nor given herself to
nor been recruited by love but become all polymath love's
androgynous advocate) yes, cruelly soon and without (at the
time) explanation, I had no fiancé. But it was to be twenty-
three years before I came out here and heard the reason.

"Now tether the horse to that gate and help me down off
this seat and we will go up there to see."

"Yessum," said Henry. He obeyed. He came round to her
side of the phaeton and reached for her small cold hand before speaking again. "See what?"

"We will see what is living up there in that house," said
Miss Louisa.

"In that house? Isn't it — ?"

"No. Hiding in it. For two years. Something has been living hidden up there in that house."

V

THE WINDOW WAS OPEN beyond Ira, snow on its raised
sash and a padding of snow on the sill, into which he had
buried his bare slender arms, heedless of if not actually

savoring the cold, as he leaned forward out into the iron New England dark of the quad, breathing the brittle cold air in slow draughts. Henry watched him from the table, watching or at least sensing the warmth of the room ebb as it sluiced around Ira's small body to free itself through the dark rectangular vacancy and into the Cambridge night, exchanged for the faint snow-muffled murmur of a few passing conversations and the gunmetal smell of chilled railings and fences and the cold. In front of Henry on the table lay the creased letter, under the lamp's squat cone of yellow (not the only light in the room but the only one strong enough to generate real brightness if not heat amid the high chambered ceiling and smudge-colored walls of the dormitory room, the only one bright enough by which to read), just as under the blanket of his bed in the next room lying casually concealed was the loaded Colt service revolver that had belonged to his grandfather. And in his father's fine slurred familiar hand the mechanical 'Hadrian Dec 17 1913 Miss,' the almost as mechanical 'My dear son' and the rest sloping headlong and elliptical toward no particular end, no conceivable object of haste, out of the same dead summerdusk, rank of wistaria and tobacco and fireflies evoked and attenuated across all the strange cold Northern miles into this strange cold room, strangely cohabited by one Yankee Jew and one confused Mississippi boy-man tortured by family and the idea of family, who just an hour earlier had finally made up his mind that he must and would kill himself:

My dear son,
Miss Louisa Sterne was buried today. She remained in the fever for more than a week and yesterday morning she died without regaining coherence if that is the word for a woman whose conscious life concocted from such various parts of petulance,

fantasy, vanity or call it pride and that furious willful female obscurity partook of so little coherence in the actual living, and without pain they say, who safely cannot know, and have surely forgotten or overlooked that if there dawned ever a day of her whole muted hysterical sentence on this earth through which she existed without pain it must either have been long before that one on which she first appeared in this town thirty years ago, or today; but perhaps that was their point. Perhaps she did in fact die *without* pain just in the sense that we enter *within* say a house of bereavement and pay our respects so they are called to the lump of cold fast-souring once-human beef and then depart *without*. Because man is born out of pain into helplessness and dies through pain into void and the best he can hope for is dispatch or postponement. But she who had spent a short empty life in waiting throughout thirty long years would have had nothing to gain now but from dispatch. So perhaps in her fevered raving last moments of if they do not wish to call suffering then at least they would not dare to call peace yesterday she did indeed die without pain, though —

— the letter having crossed those same darkened miles of strangeness and railroad and now ice that had brought Henry himself away from his own family and place and the summerdusk smells, the tobacco and the wistaria and the camphorous pungence of cotton-bound womanflesh, the September evening that would prepare him so well, she had told him, to sit in this room in the North.

"Of course," Ira said, turning. "So this is Private Sterne, this wandering Jew, this Robinson Crusoe who found himself somehow adrift and at large in the Confederate army, he was so revolted or chastened or maybe just shamed by what he saw his superior officers, that's the colonel whom he probably did not even know and the corporal whom he probably knew all too well, by what he saw his superiors trying (and for that matter succeeding) to bring off in the name of the Cause and the guise of a legitimate military risk for which he the private had probably not in the first place volunteered—namely, this cold-blooded murder—that whatever contortions of sectional sentiment or labored principle had carried him into that peculiar affiliation were revoked, canceled, ruptured, and he lit out on his horse, this Private Sterne, without a parting look back to old Johnston or Vicksburg or anything else, no longer a Rebel he, but now twice (at least) outcast, double-pariahed, a traitor himself to the Rebellion; and he wound up in Illinois. But that wasn't enough. After twenty years of the quiet life up there in Rock Island running his Monkey Ward outlet or sewing machine agency or whatever, after twenty years of rankling memory and hatred, sure and of course guilt, it wasn't enough but that our Sterne must send his only begotten daughter back down, not only to the state of (and here I might as well say state of siege, mightn't I?—or of confusion or ignorance, or yes, perhaps in a way even innocence?) Mississippi, but to the very town in which Surrat just happened (of course Sterne knew: he had made inquiries) to have a son of his own at school, and so the rest is history. Not stinting, our Sterne, to sacrifice his own daughter on the crude piney altar of a Southern finishing school, he managed to sever the son from the father and thereby unmade the very man, this Colonel and soon to be Governor Surrat, who stood convicted, to Sterne's own personal knowledge and yes perhaps shared festering guilt, of the ugliest of hypocritical treacheries. But now wait. What I still don't get is this. How did Surrat himself know? When his son returned to the house over that Christmas of '85 with the blushing young Yankee Cressida, she the kerosene lamp of his heart's night, and Surrat saw her and saw what she was, how did he know that his game was up? How did he make the connection? He must have seen this Private Sterne, the despised common flunky, when Sterne had been put up to handling his grimy deed back there at Vicksburg, he must have known the man after all, sure, he must have known him by face and name if not by character as a bodyguard or an orderly around headquarters, who had perhaps performed chores of this ilk for the Colonel before. Of course, this Private Sterne, he was one of the Colonel's own boys, probably came with him out from Virginia when Surrat had been transferred back, this one no Mississippian at all, but a Tidewater tea-merchant's bookkeeper or something, until Surrat went too far, and tried murder. Of course. Because how else could Surrat know, when she turned up on his doorstep, that his son had come under the spell of a girl who was daughter to a man in whose power it lay to destroy him. That's right, isn't it? Isn't that right?"

"No," Henry said. "She wasn't the private's daughter. Uriah James was her father."

The chimes had long since rung for ten. Ira, his face reposed, unsurprised though almost sullen, continued to stare in silence, his dark whorled mat of small headcurls more like a Negro's than like Henry's flax, his features acute and birdlike and anything other than negroid, his sharp beardless jaw and dark eyes and tight poutish lips, and his body delicate angular and loosely hung as a marionette's, and especially his small but distinctive nose, an arched narrow blade like the beak of a hawk, erect, almost exclamatory in the midst of the otherwise sober wry face. Ira's hands were thrust down into front pockets of the flannel bathrobe, his back to the still-open window, as Henry waited for him to speak, to say something, while Henry himself thought, No, I have heard it too many times. I have been over it too many times, Henry thought, thinking again of the ancient varicose and despairing spinster wrapped like a towsack of old rustling cobs and husks in her faded black cotton dress (and neither much smaller nor bigger than Ira, now dangling before him) close and oppressive though sweatless at his side on the seat of the phaeton that night who, defying belief and appearance, had as he knew (or so he was told) once, in a vague Northern state which Henry had never seen nor bothered to try to imagine, been a young girl.

"Her mother was an Illinois woman," Henry said. "Uriah had married again when he reached the North, after he made his escape, his disappearance, his change of places and names and loyalties. He had traded identities with the corpse, the Private Sterne (I don't know what the first name was or whether he used it because she always spoke of him as Uriah, never Father nor what she may have grown up hearing Northerners call him nor anything else) who had died and been buried or rather consumed by the crawfish in Uriah's stead; then he rode up the River, and started fresh. It must have been near the end of the War, or afterward, that he married her mother. I don't think Uriah ever fought for the North but I couldn't say how he avoided it, probably bought his way out, though where he could have got that kind of money so quickly, leaving home with only another man's clothes and another man's horse (and a poor man's at that), I don't know. Maybe he went West first and earned something, or maybe he just hid out until it was over and there was no need to make explanations. I don't know. Then he settled down to a new life and family in Rock Island, maybe partly because it was on the River (I think) and he could get news, but the second wife didn't last him much longer than had the first. She gave him a child, a daughter, and they named her Louisa. Miss Louisa told me that much herself. Then she stopped."

"All right," said Ira. "Go on."

"l said she stopped."

"I heard you. Stopped what? Stopped giving him children, or just daughters, or stopped being his wife and her mother or living in Rock Island, Illinois, or anywhere? Stopped breathing? Stopped what?"

"She stopped talking," said Henry. "Miss Louisa. She stopped telling it. This was after we left the house. That was all she would say. She just stopped."

"Oh," Ira said. "That night after you and the old lady. After you left the house. I see. All right. Go on. So Uriah raised her himself in a house without mother or wife or love but only the minute calculation of a man so excruciatingly patient in his vengefulness that she could not bring herself to talk about it (and by whom she herself alone of all gullible man- and womankind was gullible and unlucky enough to earn betrayal: that's what she meant, when she wouldn't absolve him, wasn't it?) and sent her South not for an education or even a finish but as the unwitting collection agent against a bad debt. Go on. And it worked—"

"—and it worked just as Uriah must have hoped," Henry said, "if even he could have hoped for so much: she met the son toward whom I guess in some guarded way Uriah had already alerted her interest, and they were drawn to each other, falling in love with the magnetic inevitability of two halves of the same ancient fossilized bone fit back into place or two twins reunited, spirit to spirit and cell to cell, and so before either of the fathers knew what was what and could stand off at a distance rubbing his hands in consternation or malicious approval, she and Chamberlain Surrat were talking about marriage."

"But it wasn't to be—"

"—but it wasn't to be because Uriah had made a miscalculation along the way somewhere whether of fact or of character wasn't clear and when Surrat met her and paired the name Sterne with the familiar (but not, as my father thought, Jewish) features, he understood at once what was up, and made his choice, losing a son to avoid gaining a daughter. It was Christmas Eve, after the turkey carcass had been taken away by the candlewax butler and the pies I suppose sampled and pushed aside and there was only the three of them. Ordinarily they might have taken brandy and Havanas there at the table and her looking on demurely drinkless and smokeless, with maybe a cup of tea. But instead Surrat merely said 'You will excuse us, I'm sure,' and led Chamberlain into the library, closing the door. And probably Chamberlain still assuming it was just the question of a financial or land settlement, a wedding gift. Until Surrat announced to the son that he could not marry her, this girl, who was the daughter of a traitor, an old enemy, and his mother's first husband."

"So he rode off—"

"Wait!" Henry said. "—Yes. So Cham rode off that night for no one knew where leaving not the least word to her about why he had gone or for how long or what had been said or why he believed it must be the truth or how that could so influence him even assuming it were. And she, left a stranger alone in the house with only Surrat to give her the news: there would be no wedding. So small wonder she turned out the way she is, was, more than a little embittered and—"

"—and more than a little crazy—"

"—all right all right, and more than a little stunted, maimed. Bewildered. Small wonder it took twenty-three years to get her back out there, anyway. Now if you want me to tell it, you're going to have to allow me to tell it."

"Of course," Ira said. "Go on. You tell it. Meanwhile she lived in her cottage giving lessons in china and piano-painting for sixty-six years without ever hearing—"

"—for twenty-three years without ever hearing, that's right, a single word more from Chamberlain Surrat; and yet she continued to love him. Yes, she still loved him, or at least she believed that she did, which in two people possessing and taking for granted each other may be quite different things but in such cases as this of loss, separation, blind devoted abeyance, must amount I would guess to the same. She lived the belief that she still loved him (she lived in fact little else) and so it was for her (as far as it went) the truth. She may have hated him too, yes, alternately or simultaneously, cursing the memory of his fine boyish arrogant unaged features so firm in her mind that they seemed to mock her own descent into cronehood, and the irremediable surrender they had extracted from her, no less than the merciless brusque unanswered question Cham had left yawning behind, a pit across which she must step every day of her life—"

"—until she went out there—?"

"—until she went out there five years ago. Because, ignorant of love as she confessed herself, she had never been told that it could come to an end," Henry said.

"So in bitterness and what might be described as the state of protracted intransitive (having no object) love and a dulled stupefaction that lingered dormant like malaria she lived through the almost twenty-five years of suspense and then the five more simply of waiting, and stopped waiting only in time to die. She was going to Illinois, Father says: but they found her in a ditch this side, I mean that side, of Holly Springs.

"Bitterness they believed, we did, the town did, toward Joseph Surrat: but that was wrong. Bitterness is a curious two-edged emotion and she never felt toward Surrat anything other than pure hatred. Her bitterness through those years was toward Cham, whom she loved and had been renounced by and did not understand. Imagine, no word during those twenty-three lonely years, not a shamefaced in-adequate note, not a hasty scrawled 'Regrettably, I cannot even explain why,' not a rumor of an excuse carried second-hand by strangers who happened to be traveling through Hadrian. Nothing. Chamberlain Surrat disappeared from her life as though dead, disappeared from the town as though a late unaccounted casualty in the same war that had ended the life of Uriah James, twenty years earlier. And so where could she turn for that answer, that explanation? Not to Joseph Surrat, the very embodiment of those sinister forces that had colluded to thwart her dreams and dismantle her hopes, and the one man in Mississippi who must have known. Not to flight, not to Rock Island, not back to her own father who (she had learned this much by then, it seems) had betrayed her in pitiless expenditure toward his selfish re-venge. No. And not—"

"Of course," Ira said, interrupting again, "because he had told the Illinois woman nothing. She knew no more about where Uriah had come from than the first wife knew where he had gone. He was the mystery man of the whole affair, wasn't he, his life foreshortened on either end: seen from one angle, having no future beyond Vicksburg, and from the other, no past before it. Uriah James. Even his name, two front halves. Like a man facing himself in a mirror.

"Jesus, the South," Ira said. He had approached the table, was leaning once more over his stick-like arms and slow spi-dery hands, smiling at Henry. "It's beautiful, isn't it? It's bet-ter than the theater, isn't it? It's better than *Alice in Wonder-land*, isn't it? It's no wonder you have to come away now and then, isn't it?"

Henry did not answer. He had let his eyes fall onto the rec-tangle of creased paper bathed by the lamp's yellow. He rested his gaze there, not to read or reread or seek rebuttal among his father's fine sloping tired words, but in retreat, silent withdrawal, regarding it with a weary stare that was at the same time helpless and accusatory.

"Sure," Ira said, "he had told the Illinois wife, while she lived, nothing. And he told the Illinois daughter even less. You were right about that. The first she had heard of it—your old Miss Louisa—the first she had known of the whole nasty treason and Vicksburg and adultery business was after the marriage that didn't happen, after that Christmas out there, after the pies and the candlewax and the little father-son conference. After Cham had lit out. Which means it must have been Surrat himself who told her. She was ignorant. I'll say she was ignorant," Ira did say. "She had been born and bred and nurtured in ignorance not just of love and the race of men but of that one particular man who happened to style himself among his other fleeting personas as her father. She didn't know him beyond a stranger. She had no inkling that Uriah had been married to someone before her mother, did she? Nor that he had escaped through a gambit of murder (or call it self-defense) and disfigurement of the corpse, with another man's name, which she now bore and believed it to be rightfully her own. Did she? And who knows but that he might have even allowed her to grow up thinking she was a Jew. Because he had gone West, that's right, had spent the last years of the War trapping beavers in Utah or doing clockwork in San Francisco or breaking horses and selling them to the Union cavalry in Kansas more likely, and what Mississippian showed in his speech was easily enough lost, shucked off like so much cornhusk and a new accent assumed, because he was a man of parts, this Uriah. Sure. Then he came back as far as Rock Island to settle and married again for love or to forget but soon found himself with a daughter and no wife, remembering. Because here's where I part ways with you," Ira said. "I don't believe he came back there to find a strategic spot on the River and pricked up his ears toward north Mississippi and took the first woman who would have him and married her and got a child on her, hoping for a girl, all to his nefarious premeditated ends. No. Because that's not only unbelievable, you see: it's unnecessary. Uriah was still no more than about twenty-five years old now, remember, wasn't he? and my guess is he was still confused, he had spent a few pretty confused years after Vicksburg out there in Kansas wondering how it had happened to him and what he should think or do about it, if anything. My guess is he came back to Rock Island after those years because it was civilization so to speak and he wanted a woman, another one, and he found one that he was interested in and soon loved or thought he loved at least as well as the childhood sweetie who had stuck the knife in his back, down there in Mississippi. He was older now, remember, more mature, and he had married the first one on the rebound from losing his momma and finding himself an eighteen-year-old orphan getting ready to go fight and die in a war, and no telling what sort of vicious tricks his emotions had been playing on him back then. So he may not have been all that broken up to be rid of her. The deceit, the deceit and betrayal (not to mention, of course, the attempted homicide) were what rankled, I'll bet, the betrayal not just by the young bride but even more so by the best friend and mentor. The loss of what love he thought he had found was maybe the least of his cares. Then he met the Illinois woman, you see, and this time it was really a woman instead of a girl, a wife instead of a sweetheart, she possibly even two or three years older than him and on the plain side but a strong tender female, a sturdy Midwestern prairie homemaker more like the boardinghouse matron, his mother, than the finishing-school mademoiselle he had married first, and he loved her, this new one, he really did, and they made a home and a family, and she by her tranquil force helping to smooth down the serrations of painful memory (for that matter he may have told her the whole thing: in one confessional outpouring of his bigamous secret he may have told her, she accepting the burden and thus cleansing him temporarily of it) and then she died. She may have died of the fever, suddenly, or a slower disease, consumption or smallpox or something that left her to grow steadily weaker and her eyes sunken and knowing, for as long as eight or ten days, and each of them watching the other recede from their grasp, understanding perhaps what it would mean to Uriah's own rehabilitation when she was gone. But here's a better idea still: she died in childbirth. Sure. And that's why he hated his own daughter. That's why he had no use for her but as an instrument of revenge.

"So Uriah raised her for sixteen years there in Rock Island while running not the sewing machine agency come to think of it but the town livery stable, just like his father, now that all the clattering hoofclaps and heady equestrian bravado had been purged from his system, and opened the vault of his past ever again neither to her nor to anyone else. And all right now, finally, yes: the design. Still little more than a vague rancorous grudge, beginning to grow and take form side by side with and as though twin brother to the girl, the living daughter, this darker thing born not out of his first aggrieved rage but in the later vacuum, the slow despair. A design that grew tumor-like to its fullness of terminal malevolence. Malevolent, yes, that was the word for him then: a strange formidable fierce inaccessible man whom neither Rock Island nor his own daughter could fathom, wishing evil for no other reason than its own sake. And so we can imagine how he would have felt pleasure, a bilious satisfaction rather than any more tender emotion, when word reached him, as it must have, that Ruth Surrat formerly James formerly Cullum had died, way down there in Mississippi, leaving a husband and a son. In fact, I'll bet it was only then (despite what the old lady claimed to you later), when that bit of news woke him from five or six years of restless impotent dreamlife, that the tumor had its inception. That he really commenced scheming.

"But of course it would take another decade or so for that tumor to swell to its fullness. He had himself a daughter, yes, a motherless little girl, but not yet a tool of revenge. He had to wait, while she grew.

"Then finally little Louisa was sixteen. And he told her one day to pack up her few home-sewn dresses and her hairbrush and needlework hoop and a volume of Scott and whatever little else she may have possessed, because she was going away to school, to be finished (finished?—he didn't lie to her, for once, when he said that) and he put her aboard the train thrusting a basket of fruit into her hand and maybe touching a perfunctory kiss to her bewildered but still unwrinkled brow as the train chuffed and began to pull out for that small Southern town where the son whom Uriah had never seen of the man he hoped to destroy was now attending the University, Uriah sending her off, launching her into the blue like a blind deadly projectile, practically shooing her out of his life while knowing full well that the chance she would have the occasion, the self-possession or even the inclination to beguile the son and thereby set him, Uriah, into power over the father was little more likely to bring him his desired result than if he had simply stood on a bluff outside Rock Island and fired a deer rifle toward Mississippi. And there you have the measure of his disdain for her. The fact of its having against every probability brought the desired result after all will never change that: his readiness not merely to use her, to sacrifice her, his only child, but if need be to squander her. It was, at best, a speculative venture. Yes, no wonder she hated him. No wonder she hated him and everything else.

"But still she knew nothing of why she was there and probably scarce understood why she was anywhere, an unwanted half-orphan outsider in a dreary vicious small world of female adolescent xenophobia, and Jesus I'll bet they made it hell for her, until near the end of the first year when her luck suddenly broke (whether from bad to good or from rotten to truly abysmal depends on whether you take the shorter or the longer view) and she found what she believed was the answer to all of her unspoken questions: it was called love. And she not only fell for it, I mean into it," Ira said, "tumbling headlong like the thirsty friar discovered drowned and smiling and literally pickled in a vat of monastic brandy, she went further, almost as though the exile back up there in Illinois were working her arms and legs and her heart on the ends of a puppeteer's strings, and became—how did she put it?—all polypoid love's amphibious advocate?"

"No," Henry said, "all—"

"Until she went out there that Christmas with her intended to talk, so they both thought, of love and soft ethereal nothings and maybe a little hard unethereal newlyweds' cottage on the north forty of Surrat's land, and the dread Puppeteer up in Rock Island or wherever He stays pulled the right string at the critical moment and her luck turned again, and finally. Uriah, of course, would not have known it at the time and it may have taken him some months to find out since with what she had now learned from Surrat she was back at the barracks in Lesbos with no more intention of ever returning North to that ogre in the guise of a benevolent if not loving father who had so misused her than of moving in with Joseph Surrat as housekeeper.

"Because Surrat must have had proof," Ira said. "He had to have had proof of some kind or he would not have convinced Cham and certainly would not have convinced her. He needed some morsel or token of proof to support what he claimed—that her father in fact was a liar, a skilled impostor, a traitor who had deserted Cham's own mother twenty years earlier and must still be capable of anything. And Surrat had it. What was it, that proof? Think now, what could it have, must it have been, that would have converted both Cham away from her and her away from her father? Not papers or letters or sworn affidavits or old Civil War pistols or pathology reports, no, but something simple, it had to be simple and bald and irrefutable. Sure, that's right, a picture. It was a picture, a cameo photograph in a small opal locket, and the face was Uriah's. Cham's mother had owned it; Uriah himself had given it to her before he rode off to war with your grandfather, and she wore it for that newlywed year and-a-half until the waiting got to be too much for her, and then put it out of her sight. But it was never lost. And then when Surrat saw your Miss Louisa and that face which you say wasn't Jewish the first Christmas, and recognized her, he knew he must find it again, the cameo locket; and he did. He bided his time, he waited a whole year, but when the affair reached that point so threatening to his ambitions and to the whole edifice of convenient forgetfulness and deceit upon which he had built a life, he played it, his trump card. He took Cham into the library and showed the locket to him and said, 'You see. You cannot doubt that she is his daughter. And he wants only to ruin me, us, by her.' And so Cham was gone. And then Surrat displayed it also to her, whether out of pity or an excess of malevolence equal only to Uriah's, who knows, who will ever know, and said, 'His name then was Uriah James. He grew up here, we all knew him. He married my late wife, and deserted her, while hardly more than a boy. I fought beside him in the War, but he turned traitor. Perhaps youth or confusion or fear might excuse him. I do not judge. We all thought he was dead.' And she saw that it was indeed her father. So Uriah, back up in Rock Island, never heard from her again. Isn't that right?"

"Yes," Henry said.

"So he wouldn't have known about that, Uriah wouldn't have, but he could have guessed, from what she had already written him of the imminent visit and her and Cham's intention to publish banns. And if Uriah did not care to guess, then the news eventually came to him: Chamberlain Surrat had broken with his father, and with his fianceé also, and disappeared. It may have been less than Uriah had hoped for, may even have left him to despair that he had failed on the very brink of success, not knowing (as he must not have known; the messenger, whoever it was, cannot have brought him that bit of information) just what he had cost Joseph Surrat, if not the Governorship. No, he would have sat up there in the smithshop of his livery stable, feeling more bitter and thwarted than ever, looking on from afar and maybe reading of the inauguration a month after the fact in an old Jackson newspaper that came to him, as Joseph Surrat his erstwhile friend, cuckolder and now blood enemy entered upon the Governorship of Mississippi, and believing himself a failure, Uriah, a self-defeated old man who had spent the only fruit of his life, his own child, in a mean cunning gambit that fell short of its mark to leave him frustrated, impotent and alone: not suspecting he had succeeded so well that this was in fact a description of Surrat rather than or as well as of himself."

"No," Henry said.

"No what?"

"No, he never believed he had failed," Henry said. "He

never believed they would marry. He never believed that Surrat would let it happen, even if that meant losing Cham."

"Why not?"

"Because he believed Cham was his own son," Henry said. "Because he never did know about that October when Surrat came home." After a moment Henry added: "And so it would have been incest."

Wait a minute, you think.

"Wait a minute," said Ira. "For God's sake wait."

VI

IT WAS LATE NOW. The window was closed above the bleak night-blue emptiness of the quad, admitting neither those tag-ends of overheard speech which had long since died away nor the pungence of cast iron frozen almost to the point of spontaneous fracture, but the harm had been done, the room was already cooling toward that stage where about one A.M. there would be only enough heat in the radiators to keep the pipes from calling out several loud final clanks of self-piteous exasperation and then freezing solid. Henry sat hunched at the table, his hands clutched in his pockets as though he were trying to hug himself warm or control his body's deep un-willed impulse to shudder, and watched his breath vaporize faintly into the room before him. Soon the chimes would ring for midnight, twelve notes melodious and grandiloquent together yet each knell direct, clear and economical as a gun-shot across cold miles.

"So this Private Sterne and the corporal, this — " Ira did not even pause, slacken, interrupting himself at full stride to in-vent the name: " — this Corporal Drangley, sure, they were summoned one afternoon near the end of the siege to the colonel's tent, that same Colonel Surrat who had made them his scurvy entourage coming out from Virginia, away from the tea merchant and the Richmond tool-and-die shop turned munitions factory where Drangley had once fed a furnace, sure, and the grinding disciplined warfare of Lee, and who had given them good horses and seen to it they got headquarters rations instead of the standard enlisted man's bivouac fare and had kept them aside from the dirty work of night picket duty for special errands (and maybe had promised to take them back with him to—what is it, Julian? Domitian? Caligula? yes, of course, Hadrian—and set them up as overseers commanding two or three dozen slaves on his land after the War, if after the War there would be such thing as slaves, such thing as his land), this same Colonel Surrat called them before him and said, probably not for the first time in that particular tone, "I have work for you." And they knew what he meant.

"Not what he thought, mind you, but meant, intended, just as far as their limited part of the intrigue was concerned. Because Surrat wouldn't have told them the truth, anything but that, who by lack of sophistication call it or their cheap-bought moral indifference neither needed nor wanted the truth, and wouldn't have known what to do and so probably wouldn't have done any differently if they'd had it; but with whom it would not have been safe. No, what he told them was better, because simpler, cleaner. 'I suspect Trooper James of treason,' Surrat said. 'I don't wish to accuse him and ruin him, not yet, not without positive proof, since this man has been like a son to me. Time and events may weigh harshly against my judgment. I accept that chance. But I am sending you with him this time, to watch. At the first sign of suspicious behavior, you must kill him. We will say he died honorably. I know I can trust you.' And then Uriah, called to the tent later that evening, and given the sealed letter.

"So at dawn the next morning they—or no, wait, cancel that," Ira said. "They would have left immediately, wouldn't they? Surrat was too far committed now to endure any delay, any occasion for miscue or discovery. So the three of them must have ridden out of camp that midnight, under cover of darkness, Uriah and Sterne and our Corporal Drangley. Headed for Vicksburg again, unbeknownst to the rest of the army, unbeknownst to your grandfather probably who had seen Uriah summoned by Surrat and not return and must have assumed he was staying to share a bottle in the comfort and light of a staff officer's tent with his old friend and probably envied him, unbeknownst even to Joe Johnston (despite what Uriah believed of that letter he was carrying, supposedly over the general's signature) on the three fresh mounts with only light saddlebags and two days of dry rations, since there would be no stopping to cook, no fires built, only brief wary interludes of rest more for the horses than for the men during the next sixty hours and—how far?—yes, hundred or so miles. And Uriah in front, leading the little group off into that maze of thickets and streambeds and dirt crossroads and enemy scouts, which he knew by now as well as anyone, thinking nothing of leaving his back exposed temptingly to the pair of scrofulous lackeys (at least until they were far enough out of camp for something to happen, for his doubts, if he had doubts, to open their dark blossoms), maybe riding forward ahead of them some distance, impatient, annoyed by the inept (that Richmond foundry cannot have prepared Drangley much better than, or even as well as the tea merchant's back room did Sterne, for spending long days and nights in the saddle: the hours of paperwork at least might have hardened Sterne's backside) and unnecessary companions Surrat had burdened him with, through the whole of the first night, maybe thinking and stewing and silently grousing upon it, wondering how Surrat could be so wrongheaded as to imagine it would make the chore easier, safer, or even simply more probable of success, begrudging the two other riders as an increase not of net manpower nor firepower nor certainly brainpower nor potential survivors but only of sum total target area exposed to enemy rifles, until maybe around noon of the next day, sure, they had pulled up in a small willow grove to water the horses and Uriah and Sterne lay down to catnap while Drangley stood watch and Uriah still grousing inwardly as he pulled the hat over his eyes and prepared to release body from mind for a few minutes of sleep when it all shifted slightly before him and came into terrifying alignment. Of course. He didn't move. No, he didn't unfold his arms, didn't even attempt to slide the hat off his face and see if he were already too late. He just lay there, and knew. Think of it," Ira said. "His body reacted, gathering about the pores like plucked chickenflesh, a chill and horrified puckering, as though warning him in slow shrill futility on the very moment of being infected with smallpox.

"Something about Surrat the night before, something unnatural in his manner, maybe a difference Uriah had sensed but not consciously noticed when he and Surrat were first reunited at Jackson weeks earlier, maybe even something as far back as the young wife's sea-change, that December when Van Dorn burned the Hadrian depot, something or other finally tripping the lever for Uriah to come wise. Who knows what it was. Not the old lady, not you and not me. Probably not even Joseph Surrat. Or maybe he did know: maybe Surrat himself tripped the lever, intentionally, slipping a grim hint into that last conference the night before, planting it in Uriah's mind, prematurely secure in the conviction that given the letter and his departure with Drangley and Sterne, Uriah's fingers were already firmly inserted into the Chinese handcuffs. So Uriah lay there, that lovely June morning beneath the willows in sweet Mississippi, and understood he was marked to die. It was the watershed of his life. He raised the hat slowly. Drangley was still standing guard. Sterne was still sleeping.

"That day Uriah rode second, giving Drangley the lead, careful not to arouse their suspicion by insisting he bring up the rear. Of course there was still Private Sterne at his back, free to pause in the saddle at any moment of Sterne's choosing and level and aim the Colt service revolver and fire neatly between Uriah's shoulder blades, though Uriah must have reflected as he rode that with luck he might hear the click when the hammer was cocked back and so dive off to the ground and get his own pistol drawn while the horse's rear end and belly protected him from a second shot or that it might be done sloppily and he only receive an arm wound yet if it were done properly as he knew it could be and as he himself would have done it, he would simply be dead; but he was betting on Private Sterne. Because he believed that Sterne would not pull a trigger cold on a man's back, at least not alone, not without Drangley beside him firing at the same instant and dwarfing his own act to mere complicity. Because this Private Sterne was not just another like Drangley, no, either more of a coward or less of a bastard, but not the same. And Uriah had seen that. He was only a private, for one thing, while Drangley was a corporal, the ranking member of their little cadre, and if there is any class of men who by self-definition are shameless and eager and sycophantish and willful enough to undertake anything yet by plain limitation of ability or vision capable of accomplishing but very little, next to nothing, it must be those who in time of war rise to the rank of corporal. Drangley was a corporal, and Sterne the sum and extent of his command. Drangley was in the War to fight not for a principle of liberty which he had never enjoyed nor a fictive ideal of jasmine and mint and verbena which he had never worshiped nor an economic system in which, being the Southern proletarian, he did not participate nor even so much against the specter of free Negroes, but against strangers. Sure, Drangley had seized the chance to go off and shoot strangers, legally, whose faces if he had time to see them he probably would not have liked, and because opportunity (so he believed before he saw how the supposedly democratic regimental elections invariably resulted in the old homelife's planters and aristocrats being chosen to the colonelcies and majorities) would be more fluid in a Confederate army than at the Richmond foundry. While Sterne on the other hand had joined up out of misguided gratitude to the city and state where he had stepped off a boat and found work commensurate to his education or because someone had told him it was the same question Washington and Jefferson had fought for eighty years earlier and he knew the names or because the women and old men and wounded left behind in Richmond were beginning to look at him disapprovingly and the tea merchant had dropped a strong hint. So with the failed Bonapartist Beauregard for a commander and Drangley for a companion he learned how to scrounge, and to loot, and to burn, and even how to kill; but not yet how to murder. He was a little man with wide dark eyes, this Sterne, you can just see him, and a small dark beard that he shaved off because the hill and plateau farmers in his regiment were suspicious of Vandykes on privates, leaving his face looking naked and tallowy and as though surprised in its bath. And a head of curled hair that Drangley probably hated in secret as much as he hated the Negroes or strangers. In fact, Drangley would have been happy to kill Sterne himself, given a reason, or even just an occasion, though he didn't need to because he was the corporal and Sterne was a private under him, and thus Drangley had something of the same jealous regard for him that a planter has for a slave, and by now anyway they had grown used to each other. So Uriah rode second, between them, betting on Sterne and those wide quiet ambivalent eyes which after a year of infantry warfare bore little shadow of scruple or qualm but which in Drangley resembled gray solid nubs of muzzle-load lead. And by late afternoon they were half way to Vicksburg.

"They stopped again, near a deep lazy creek which they had got close enough to the River by now to call a bayou. It crooked its way through a half mile of bottomland pasturage but they came up to it from the woods, dense florid and almost tropical here, draped over with Spanish moss or whatever that—what? scuppernong, yes—draped with wild scuppernong vine over the trees and the bushes and the ground like a weighty hampering blanket of specious hopes or guilty memories so that the horses could hardly lift their hooves through it without stumbling, and they were careful to stay out of sight from the farmhouse. Emerging, they watered the horses and drank. The creek was warm, murky, probably had cattle wallowing and fouling in it upstream, but they were thirsty, and not about to risk meeting a Yankee patrol just to find clean cold water. Maybe Uriah abstained, knowing the ways of this countryside better than those two, knowing the feculent poisons that dwelt in such a stream, knowing the distance yet to Vicksburg and the needs of his own body, maybe contenting himself with a corner of dry cornbread or a stem of grass: although such caution was undeniably frivolous, moot, knowing too as he did by then the whispering proximity of death. Still, I see him standing there dry, ride-parched, quietly disdaining to touch the least drop, with that mindless maniacal fidelity to good habits by which the suicide brushes his teeth and his hat before going out to leap off the bridge, while the others drank," Ira said. Henry barely flinched. "Then Sterne wandered modestly back into the woods to relieve himself, and Drangley, jumping the creek, declared he would hike up through a peach orchard on the side of a gentle hill rising opposite, to make a reconnaissance toward the road. Uriah was left alone.

"He might have been fooled. Given this easy and obvious chance for escape, he might have stood like a salt pillar and watched Drangley walk up the hill, wondering what to do now, whether to climb on his horse and flee, whether in fact if they left him so casually there could be any danger from which to flee after all; and maybe he suddenly felt very young and excitable and relieved. Or maybe he had no need to stand wondering what he must do: only to wait carefully. Anyway, by the time Drangley passed out of sight, Uriah was at the saddlebags. And now he would have kept the flank of his horse between himself and the orchard, so he could watch for Drangley and not be detected as he went through the bag. The hand which brought out the letter was trembling. He broke the general's waxen seal, tore it open, and read it.

"He probably lost track of the moments: felt the sharp driving blow to his back, only then heard the shot from behind and saw the horse scream and rear with a wound in its own haunch, from the same bullet that had lanced through his shoulder. He was probably not surprised, not then, not yet, releasing the letter and thinking quite clearly, as he went down or even before, 'Of course I should have known, shouldn't I,' then 'So I have been shot through the heart and will now die. This is the last thought I will have time to think,' then 'If I'm not lucky the horse will trample me,' maybe not even having time to realize that as the letter fell his own hand had moved instinctively to the pistol. So that when he discovered himself on the ground neither dead nor unconscious but only shot through the left shoulder he found that his right hand, pinned under him, was holding a loaded gun. Then the horse's leg buckled and the animal collapsed, rolling its squealing massive warm bulk down on his legs. He couldn't move. 'The final irony,' Uriah thought. And 'I have certainly had more than my share.'

"He did not even try to move, not at first. He waited. He waited another heartbeat or more, expecting the end, the true end not the false one, the second shot, to follow as quickly as the next shuddering bloodpulse had jumped through his body after he realized he was still for the moment alive. But the shot didn't come. And he remembered now that the first had been fired from some distance, thirty or forty yards, recalling lucidly that slight delay after the bullet struck and then also the volume of the report and therefrom the deducible range of the shot, and aware now that, incredibly, only a second or two or at most three had elapsed during all the new sensations and realizations since he had been wounded, so that Sterne could have only begun to close on him, even running, for the kill. Because he still believed it was Sterne. He made a pitifull floundering movement with the upper half of his body, maybe two or three times, under the horse's weight, not quite desperate but hurried and intent and careful already again now to keep his head if he could below the shield of the horse's ribs, before he got the arm free. Then he rested the pistol across the horse's rear end for a rifle bench, patting the creature and coaxing her to remain inert just a moment longer, and waited. He still believed it was Sterne, because he had not yet considered how Drangley could have pretended to go up through the orchard in one direction then circled back at the ridgetop and snuck down

into the scuppernong woods so as to come around from behind and get the jump on or at least watch Uriah undetected.
Maybe if there had been time for considering, Uriah still
wouldn't have granted even to Drangley that level of devi-
ousness. So they were both surprised. Drangley stepped into
view above the curve of the horse, eight feet away, with the
pistol drawn and cocked again and held ready at arm's length
to fire the second shot, which Drangley may have suspected
he would require but probably planned to fire anyway, required or not, into the wounded or dead body of Uriah, and
found himself looking down into not only Uriah's open alert
angry eyes but the mouth of a pistol as ready and deadly as
his own, and the moment was timeless. They were both surprised, frozen in labors of recognition that had to precede the
next conscious act, their eyes linked across the short distance
in that familiar and almost intimate instantaneous union between killer and victim, uncertain suddenly who would be
which: Uriah surprised because it was Drangley, not Sterne,
appearing unaccountably from the wrong direction as though
in sinister bifurcative defiance of physical law, Drangley surprised because from the earlier moment's smug assassin he
was demoted to one of two equal and frail duelists about to
shoot each other to death, Drangley's surprise maybe the
more extreme because he had in his smugness allowed himself the assumption that Uriah was hit through the heart, so
that he now faced the warm quickened eyes of a dead man,
taking aim. Whatever, Drangley's the more extreme, and then
on the heels of the surprise a single identical thought crackling all but simultaneously through the two minds, 'Yes, all
right, there is that but now I must squeeze this trigger
quickly immediately at once and I hope to God I have done
it by now,' Drangley's minutely the more extreme and en-
cumbering and the two pistols leveled across conversational

distance and so Uriah saw it was him and not Sterne and squeezed and even as the pistol roared Uriah could not tell whose it was until Drangley's head snapped and he went over backward, a hole where his face had been. And this time there was no need of a second shot.

"Uriah must have wrenched free of the horse by the time Sterne appeared, which cannot have been long after the first shot, only seconds enough for Sterne to get his pants up and his belt hitched and stumble out through the scuppernong. So there would have been little chance for Uriah to ambush him, making an easy end of it. Probably Sterne got as far as the edge of the woods just as Uriah prodded the horse over and rose to his feet, and Sterne saw him and saw Drangley's body and cursed Drangley fiercely and finally before turning back into the woods and scrambling for his life. Because they both knew by now there would be no returning to Johnston nor going on anywhere in safety while the other still lived. So Sterne, who had probably never shared Drangley's relish for the prospect of Mississippi and two or three dozen Negroes, who had probably been as unhappy volunteering (as it would have been called) for this chore as for the others, Sterne turned tail and ran, cursing Colonel Joe Surrat and the Confederacy and the vines that clutched at his feet as he went. And now Uriah could have taken his time, if he chose to (which, with the shoulder wound, he probably did) and collected the rifle that would have fallen from its saddle holster when the horse was shot down (which he probably did not bother to do, realizing at once that a rifle in that tangled jungle of scuppernong would be as worthless and cumbersome as a longhandle broom) so he took just his own pistol and Drangley's, tracking Sterne into the woods. It may have lasted an hour or two, the rest of the afternoon, but probably not, with Uriah losing blood from the shoulder.

"For a while Sterne tried to outrun him, to the edge of that maddening dry swamp, to a farmhouse, to the first Union camp or patrol, anywhere, stumbling, maladroit, terrified, hopeless. He may have returned a few wild shots, gulping for breath behind those buckled trees draped with their scuppernong like a house full of old furniture made ghostly beneath sheets, incapable of hunkering himself quietly down in the vines to gamble for a close shot at Uriah's back. Gun empty, he did not try to reload, his fingers were useless with palsy; he just ran on. When Uriah reached him, collapsed in the vinework, the revolver was still in Sterne's hand, forgotten. Maybe he wept, maybe he begged for mercy. Maybe he even called out forlorn to a strange, distant god, in a strange, atavistic language. Maybe he didn't. Maybe he said nothing, gave no satisfaction, did not even raise his face. Uriah shot him once through the head, using Drangley's gun. Then he carried Sterne's body back to the clearing and took its clothes. Drangley he left to be found. Sterne he threw into the creek. The water was already undrinkable," Ira said.

Henry did not even raise his face. "You couldn't enjoy it so much if you had to live with it," he said.

VII

AND NOW THEY WERE both shuddering. Ira had seated himself opposite Henry at the small table as though over a chess game. His hands, under the cone of the lamp, lay folded, now unfolded, now folded again, alternately yawning and closing graceful long fingers upon themselves with the slow rhythmic menace of courting mantids. Henry, shivering not like Ira in occasional light spasms but steadily, rackingly, even under the topcoat that Ira had fetched from the bedroom and thrown over his shoulders, fists still clenched in pockets and elbows pressed to his ribs, watched with distracted intentness the hands folding, unfolding, folding again in unconscious accompaniment to the voice.

"All right. All right," Ira said. "So Uriah had proof of his own, a fine little piece of it. His wasn't as compact and graphic as the cameo locket maybe and maybe not quite irrefutable since Surrat had been canny enough to allow for the possibility of discovery but damning testimony nonetheless, particularly in light of developments on the domestic front so soon afterward, and not only in Surrat's own handwriting but even (if Uriah had had presence of mind after he put on the other uniform and shot his horse to retrieve not just the letter but the envelope) sealed spuriously with the official signet of a full general in the army of the one-time Confederate States of America. And Uriah carried it with him when he followed the River north, through those once peaceful familiar woods which now harbored two enemy armies instead of just one (at least until he could reach Kansas and find a new set of clothes and a new story), that letter in fact the sole vestige of his earlier life, the lone physical token uniting him to the man he had been or had thought he was during twenty-three years and the home and homeland and wife and name (and, so you say he had come to believe, probably during that December when Van Dorn had him back burning his own town, son) he was leaving behind. He probably carried it inside his coat, probably had it pinned to the lining like a $20 bill in reserve for the morning's breakfast and hot bath and ticket on the first train out of town to follow the night's disastrous poker game, through the whole dismal time he spent chasing range ponies in Kansas, three years or whatever it was, hoarding it waspishly even as he wondered what in the hell he would ever do with it, all the while letting it eat out his guts like a Spartan boy's stolen fox.

(Because he continued to pay for that souvenir, that deben-
ture against vengeance, even long after the scuppernong, you
can bet on it, living [not just his own life but his daughter's]
in angry abeyance for the day of its maturation when he
might have just burnt the damn thing and forgotten. Or
tried.) Then drifting back east to Illinois where he settled and
unpinned it cherishingly from the coat to put at the bottom
of an old chiffionier drawer and hoarded it and the grudge
and the daughter for twenty years before attempting to cash
in on what he considered (with that snow-blind lack of scruple only righteousness knows) to be justly his, though Deu-
teronomy says otherwise. And in fact he did, he successfully converted it, despite what you dismiss as a slight miscalculation whether of fact or of character uncertain but
which seems to me clearly enough one of fact, and that far
from slight. Because if he believed Chamberlain Surrat was
his own son and so planned to destroy the prospective governor by encouraging an incestuous marriage or rather a po-
tentially incestuous betrothal only to explode the whole deal
by his appearance as from the grave at the appropriate, is
hardly the word, moment of the ceremony with letter in
hand, like a mad old sailor waving a brace of albatross, to
prevent his own son from marrying his own daughter under
Surrat's auspices, blessing and roof, to the delight of every
newspaper within 400 miles, then it seems to me that Uriah's
miscalculation was more than slight. Because Surrat, knowing the truth (that there was in fact no incest at all because
Cham was *not* Uriah's son), had the option of letting the
marriage happen and then taking his chances with the trou-
blesome new in-law whom everybody believed anyway was
a traitor not to mention dead and if neither of those then at
least a deserter to wife and duty despite the twenty-year-yel-
lowed scrap of sweat- and horse-scented paper this person

might brandish while hobbling ghostlike and disorderly up the center aisle of the makeshift chapel. So Uriah would have failed. Which he didn't, as we agree. Instead, Surrat relinquished first that son who was to be the price of his governorship and soon afterward that governorship itself, which he apparently found over-priced and only a daily mockery of his gullibility for having so dearly bought it, and he retired back to your town where he spent his remaining afternoons seated quietly among pigeons under the Rebel monument which we can safely assume graces your town square, both Surrat and that stone effigy of a common soldier no doubt facing south and like co-equal partners in mute adamantine befuddlement wondering where it all went wrong. And which furthermore he, Uriah, did not for a moment despair of having achieved, successfully, even while seeing the marriage forbidden and the election won. Well, maybe Uriah was an optimist. Maybe he felt lucky. Maybe he had second sight. But whose son did Surrat think Chamberlain *was*, anyway?"

"Yes," Henry said. "Surrat believed that Cham was his own."

"Right. So now wait," Ira said. "Because it occurs to me finally that we're moving too fast. It occurs to me finally that we've passed over something, someone. A very critical figure in this whole little diorama has been given short shrift. His name is Chamberlain Surrat. It occurs to me now what event in his boyhood brought on that transmogrification your father described, setting him one step aloof from Surrat's paternal wardenship, his own man while still a boy; his own parthenogenetic being. It was when he attained that treacherous moment of adolescence old enough to count backwards to nine from the month of his own birth.

"Of course," Ira said. "Or maybe just old enough to comprehend when some obliging playmate a year or three older did the counting for him. Because in Chamberlain's case, he wouldn't have had to count very far. Because that little lady, the first wife, the fickle-hearted finishing-school daughter of the town judge, the one who whatever might have been thought as to the rest was undeniably Chamberlain's mother, she had been growing ripe as a fig all through the siege of Vicksburg. Sure. I had pictured her as a frail discreet wispy intense little double-dealer, back there outside of Hadrian keeping her eyelids lowered modestly and her hands folded on her lap and letting the menfolk thrash it out, but that was wrong, that was a visual fallacy, because she was already fat like a harvest honeydew by July, wasn't she? Hands on her lap? She had had no lap for months. She was obviously and lewdly pregnant when Surrat married her.

"No."

"No what? Don't tell me no. Surrat had the furlough in October of '62, right? He cashiered Uriah in June '63 and got through helping Johnston decline to save Vicksburg at the start of July, right? The old lady confirmed that Cham was born just after the fall of the city, right? Well then don't tell me no because any fool with ten fingers and a rabbit's grasp of biology can see clearly that—"

"No. He married her afterward," Henry said. "After Cham's birth. He couldn't get back until August."

"Oh. All right then. So he married her afterward. And made Cham legal and she died and Cham grew to where he could count backwards to nine which in his case was forward to one, and discovered to his disgust that his father and mother were human. Don't we all. Only no, that still isn't enough, is it? It was more than that, a hell of a lot more than a simple case of the twinkle in Papa's eye having preceded the wedding band on Momma's finger. It was something serious. Of course. Now I see. Cham had heard for the first time of that abiding and very central fact in his life, that fact which had somehow escaped and lain fossilized in a stratum of shame inaccessible to the casual cruel archeology of playground iconoclasts. He had heard that Surrat was not, or at least might not and certainly should not have been, his father. He had heard of Uriah.

"And this time it was an adult, disinterring the story for him. Yes, an adult, it must have been. But who, or what manner of person, out of what troubled talent for evil, only God and Cham Surrat knew, and maybe neither of them understood. 'Chamberlain,' he was told, whispered to, hissed at, 'they've lied to you. Joseph Surrat is not your father.'" Ira, hunched slightly forward over his hands, his sharp arc of nose slicing keel-like into the lamplight, hissed the words quietly at Henry. "'Your mother was married before. Your mother'—yes, thus besmirching forever, this filthy but credible voice, the memory of that mother who was already since his eighth year lost to the boy—" hissing: "—'your mother was married once to another man, a man you have never seen. Chamberlain. She was still married to him on the night you were conceived.'" Ira sat back. "Think of it. Like revealing to you that you are not you who you thought you were but some alien individual with the same or a different name, maybe Francis Bacon or Christopher Marlowe who has accidentally been switched as an infant into your didies and blue bonnet and pram. What would you do? Jesus, your father is not your father but a stranger; and a stranger is your father. Think of it. What would you do?"

"I don't know," Henry said. "And I don't want to think of it."

"All right," Ira said. "Maybe I don't either. Maybe none of us want to. But we *have* thought of it, of course, so it's too late for that. You have I know without asking and I have I admit and I daresay everyone has, sooner or later: looked askance and covertly some evening at dinner or as he was seated with pipe or cigar over account books at his study desk or shambling in his clumsy topcoat up a public sidewalk through full light of day to meet us, looked at that stranger who sleeps (or at least, has slept) with our mother and in whose image and likeness more than that of any other creature on earth we are supposedly concocted, and wondered mystified: How can it be? How can this man, charming or endearing or sufferable enough in his own way but certainly nothing like me, or like me as I see myself, how can he in fact be my father, the single male human adult whose foibles and flaws and very blood I have directly inherited? It must be cosmic irony, we decide. Or it must be blind utter randomness. Or it must be a lie. And so we do, we speculate with secret benign traitorousness as to who, if our father (as logic seems to suggest) were not truly our father, might our real and more appropriate father be. Don't you believe that?"

"I don't know," Henry said. He still did not raise his face. Ira watched him. Even while they were silent their bodies trembled, their breaths in the tomblike air vaporized gently and quietly.

"You mean, it doesn't matter to you?"

Henry did not answer. "That's right. Don't say it," Ira continued. "Because I would know you're lying. I wouldn't have to read the rest of your father's letter or your reply if you write a reply to know that you yield something the same grateful uneasy ambivalent fealty to the—what did you say he does? yes, that's right, religion, he's in religion—to the Presbyterian I think it was minister down there in Hadrian as I do to a certain haberdasher in Concord. Because I could tell from the very way you fingered the envelope before opening it, the way you wondered for those few seconds what momentous event could have moved your father who probably does not write letters except to bishops and synods and shingling contractors but customarily delegates the scribal communication with offspring to your mother or rather (that's right, I'm sorry) your sister, to write you a letter at all. Because I know: you haven't seen me reading any in haberdashery handwriting, have you? No. It's not unique, and it probably hasn't even improved or got worse in generations, centuries. Take the man up in Concord, for instance, living a comfortable and mainly untroubled and in certain ways noble existence selling tie-pins and ascots and embroidered—"

"He isn't a minister," Henry said.

"He what? No, of course, he's—"

"He isn't a minister anymore," Henry said. "He's still an ordained clergyman. But he isn't a minister. Because he has no congregation to minister to, you see."

"Oh. All right, sure. But what does he do, then? What does he do now that he's not ministering? What does a clergyman—"

"He's a landowner," Henry said.

"A landowner," Ira repeated. "That's what he does."

"Yes."

"All right," Ira said. "All right. Then he's a landowner not a minister and this other up there in Concord is a haberdasher, which is to say owner of vast numbers of hats and garters which happen to be for sale, and who speaks English fastidiously but with a heavier accent than you do and who came to this state not on a train but on a boat and part of the way by horsecart as I have been told more than once out of a small wheat-growing village near the Black Sea beside which Concord is New York City. And for whom there is no greater dream than to someday grow old enough with a healthy son maybe a Harvard lawyer in Concord that he can hoist hats stick-pins moderately well-salted safe and haberdashery books all on his failing stooped honest shoulders and heave the whole business at me, saying, 'So here, not much I can give to a man who already has'—(and too polite even to say *has been given*)—'Harvard, but take it, that was done only for you,' so that I like the bloodless ingrate I must inevitably be can then duck. So you see how even we two who have only a few dozen acres of cotton or silk to fear and despise, you and I, can understand why Cham would have grown up remote."

"Yes," Henry said, raising his face.

"And that still isn't it."

"No," Henry agreed.

"No," Ira said. "Of course not. Because there is still Surrat. And the man who designed that letter, with the flick of a pen across government-issue bond sweeping Uriah helpless and defamed into exile for twentysome years, was not to be so easily scotched by one fevered town gossip. Surrat now had a choice to make. Cham had been told of Uriah (or at least that part of Uriah's story leading as far as the Johnston camp on the night of that final departure for Vicksburg) and though Cham's source for this story was only one disreputable individual, still the record was public: he could approach any adult in town and, by watching their faces as they refused to speak of it, find confirmation for what he had heard. Surrat for his part had not asked for a son, had not intended one, had not even married in time to legitimize one. But willing or nilling, a son he had. And he seems to have valued that son, not as he valued the woman he once coveted or the wife he later (let's be generous and say) loved, but abstractly, in his peculiar way, according to some invisible but carefully measured (at least so he believed, until finding himself alone in the Governor's mansion) rate of exchange. Well, this time the rate was too meager. The son, a walking and breathing fact he prized without quite knowing why, was apparently more dear than the price of keeping him. So he chose desperately. He chose (and maybe that was his blunder, throwing a lifetime of cautious prevarication into forfeit) as he never otherwise chose: he chose the truth. He sat Chamberlain down, just a boy of let's say twelve, in one of those same library chairs where they would argue and then part for life a decade later. 'What they tell you is false,' Surrat said. 'It is only partially accurate. There was a Uriah, yes. He went to the War and'—(Surrat didn't yet know any differently)—'died. But I am your father. I am your real and true father. Because your mother and I were adulterers.' Of course. And then he explained what he meant."

The chimes tolled once: a single note pulsing above darkness, austere, without musical quality, whether signaling one o'clock or half past they would have no means to judge for at least thirty more minutes.

"And so ten years," Ira resumed, tried to, but stopped. The shivering had begun to ascend through his body, rattling him irresistibly, possessing him, like a sneeze or a moment of passion, and he waited. He tightened elbows to his ribs and shoulders against his neck, letting the spasm work its course, it finally escaping him like a mangled cry or a curse, and was gone, diffused. He relaxed. Then he turned the collar of the bathrobe up about his neck.

"And so ten years," he said again. "Chamberlain growing to manhood self-contained as a desert spore, an obedient and formal and at least outwardly respectful scion and heir to the father he held at an arm's distance, accepting home, nurture, name and maybe even friendship from the man by whom he believed himself treacherously begotten on another husband's wife, but never accepting the bond of living fatherhood, whatever we've decided that is. Surrat for his part biding time, the civic widower and seemingly casual lax understanding parent, while the seeds of that ruthless (and some would believe rootless, but the old lady was right in not subscribing to such eyewash) ambition, which was soon to erupt and bloom and as quickly wilt, received their water and sunlight and bided their own clock's time until germination within him; Surrat believing that what he had paid in coin of diminished stature and rectitude, before the eyes of that son he took jealously to be his own, would justify and redeem itself, not because it happened to be the truth or because the fealty if not love of this particular child was irreplaceable to him but because he had already lost that one wife who seems to have been the only one he had ever cared to take, borrow, steal, and because he believed with the same groping naive apostasy which had led him south out of Nashville and away from the first gandygang that that morality which called one man's wife another's damnation was human-made and thus did not impress or interest him while the chain of fatherhood was somehow decreed and transcendent. Never suspecting, Surrat, that the note then signed would return to him in a few years at price of settlement far beyond the cool measured regard he received from Cham. And Uriah, at his station, drawing and sectioning out the years with fanatic patience, believing all the while that Cham was *his* son, *his* revenge. And finally she, the old lady, a girl then, suspecting nothing, measuring little, believing only in love. So it was Christmas of '85.

"And the old man sent the candlewax butler for Cham. Because Surrat had not joined the young lovers that evening for dinner or brandy or anything, like you claim. He had been alone in the library all afternoon," Ira said.

"He was deciding," Ira said.

"Because he knew she was not a Jew," Ira said. "So he wouldn't have bothered with that, despite what your father believed. He knew who she was, from the first glimpse, a year earlier. He knew from his first view of the girl's face not only that Uriah James had survived Drangley and Sterne, had somehow defied mortality and decay and the ravening crawfish that gathered to eat of and cluster on Sterne's body like goosefeathers (until it had been unrecognizable when the farmer approached close enough to the creek that his footfall sent the sudden alarmed silent cloud of creatures scuddering away from a bare skeleton which was taken to be Uriah's), but even that Uriah lived still, those twenty years later, having contracted with fate in exchange for his soul or whatever to recruit even love, the gossamer foolish insistent infatuation of this son and this daughter, to the furtherance of his hatred. Surrat knew that Uriah could ruin him, wreck his career, and would. Yet just as surely, he knew that the trump card upon which Uriah was counting as the means to destroy him, namely the incest, was nonexistent. A figment of Uriah's misinformation. So— ... I mean, but—"

Again Ira ceased. The feverish chills took hold of his delicate body like a gust among windchimes of bamboo. Across the small table, Henry was still, bundled, waiting.

"All right," Ira said. "Now I can see why you called it a miscalculation of character."

"Yes," Henry said. "Sent the butler for Cham, then, if you want. And Cham came into the library, and Surrat said to him—"

"I know: 'What I confessed to you ten years ago, about your mother and me, was a lie. I did it for love.' Or maybe, 'I did it from loneliness.' Maybe he even said, more convincingly, 'I don't know why I did it.' Sure. Then he brought out the locket. And told his son: 'So you cannot marry her, Chamberlain. Because'—"

"—'she is your sister,'" said Henry.

"Sure. Knowing that this itself was—"

"—believing that this was—"

"—the lie. The granddad so to speak of his lies. Wonderful. It couldn't have been simpler. He denied the son for whom he had already cheated and betrayed and murdered (and even so much as told the truth) just to claim as his own. Banished that son, drove him away to God only knows what desolate wintry island of bitter retirement. And was rid of him, free and clear. Joseph Surrat: governor to a million, and father to no one."

Yes," Henry said.

"Well Jesus," said Ira, "that's fine. I'm glad for him. I'm glad for them all. Now I want you to tell me just one thing more. If your grandfather never knew, though he suspected Uriah was not dead, and your father never knew and the town never knew and even she, the old lady, only found out herself after twenty-three years when body and spirit said it was too late, then why on earth did she tell you, a stranger?"

"She didn't," Henry said.

"She didn't? But you said she did. You said the old lady told you that night when you took her out there to the—"

"No. I learned it, the rest of it, that night. But she didn't tell me."

"Then who did?"

"Chamberlain Surrat."

"Oh," Ira said. "Oh. Of course." He stood. "Come on. Let's get out of this damn icebox and go to bed."

Everyone is cold. Henry and Ira prepare to retire. But you stay up.

VIII

AT FIRST, in the dark of the bedroom, it only seemed colder, as if the squat mandarin cone of lamplight had in fact loaned the outer room some puny token of inappreciable heat before Ira snapped it off, and now the iron and inexorable night surged back unabated through walls and windows and the very snowheavy bedclothing under which Henry's feet knew, like a memory beneath dark water, the revolver's shape. The gun was startlingly cold, solid and cold as paradox, slow to warm, though his soles pressed at it almost caressingly. Then the darkness itself seemed to sigh, to relax, to settle; and beneath the heavy thickness of blankets Henry's blood pulsed again, running warmer. Only the gun was still cold. He was no longer sure what he would do with it. He was no longer sure of the awful simplicity of his own pain. He felt vaguely cheated.

"The Governor's mansion at Jackson," Ira's voice said from the iron-cold darkness to Henry's right. "Versailles dragged screaming recalcitrant into existence from out of a steamy cottonwood brake."

"Yes," Henry said. "Surrat must have been miserable there."

"I certainly wouldn't want to spend my declining years there," Ira agreed, "even if it meant getting away from my family and in-laws. Of course, I wouldn't want to spend my declining or for that matter ascending years in Jackson, Mississippi, even if I could do it outside of the Governor's mansion, I guess. Even if I could do it outside of Jackson, I guess. Even if I could go back up to Hadrian and sit with the pigeons and the stone soldier, staring at Mexico. Wait. Listen. I'm not trying to be funny. I just want to understand it. Because it's different from my people. We carry our pogroms and miseries and our blindered tenacious prideful optimism around on our backs with the haberdashery books, you see. Because we don't have the land, like you do. We don't have any land, anywhere, to stand on and walk back and forth across our bad memories like a prayer rug or a swamp reclamation project that failed. We don't have that. So I just want to understand how it is. I mean, is it easier, or harder? How is it to know that the dirt under your feet, under your father's house, under your fingernails if you are a small boy or a farmer, is the very same earth that you must always remember not to forgive Sherman for having scorched, the very same sod that was trenched and thrown up to make those breastworks at Vicksburg, the very same frozen mud across which Van Dorn's horse hoofclattered into town when he came to burn Grant's stockpile of clean linen and whiskey, so that forever-more as long as your sons' sons produce sons you won't be anything but a descendant in the long line of dirt farmers who hefted a shovel at Shiloh?"

"Shiloh is Tennessee," Henry said. "You can't understand. You have to live with it. Not just on it, but with it."

"Would I then?" said Ira. Henry was silent. "Do you understand?"

"Of course," Henry said. "Yes." They breathed in the darkness. After a moment Henry said, "I think so."

"You think so," said Ira. "Fine. Fine. Then tell me this: why did she wait?"

"Why did who wait?"

"Why did the old lady wait? If she knew five years ago that it was not and would never have been incest? If she knew for the last three months everything you told me tonight? If she knew since you went out there with her in September that Cham (for whom she had already waited twenty-eight years) was living hidden alone in the house? Why did she keep waiting? Why did she wait until two weeks ago before going back out there so she could die of exposure trying to find him again and convince him that it was all right, that she still loved him, that everything between them might still happen? Your father said she was made for it. He said she had learned how. Is that all? Are you going to tell me that she knew Cham was out there yet she left him to make the next move because she had forgotten how *not* to wait?"

"No," Henry said. "She didn't know he was there. She didn't see him that night," Henry said. "She saw someone else."

"Someone else?" There was the noise of Ira sitting up in the bed. "Who?"

Henry didn't answer immediately. He could smell the camphor. Even now, with the pure alien pungence of frozen cast iron filling his nostrils, he could smell the camphor-reek of her black shawl, the fussy hermetic maidenly sweat of long-sequestered womanflesh, the rank airless clean dryrot in the very storage folds of her widow's (who was never a bride) black cotton dress, close beside him there on the phaeton's seat. He could smell the horse sweat, not wafted back to him but hanging immobile in each spatial increment (that September air was so still) and he drawn forward through it by the horse. He could hear the dry moan of the axle beneath him and the gentle suspirant hiss of the wheels spreading a layer of road dust weightless and silken and deep with the season, and the parched earth's silent agony offered heavenward to aloof and impervious stars. He could taste the dust. Now she spoke, answering the first question he dared to insert into her monologue since they had left her cottage.

"No," she said, "tether it to that gate. And we will go up there to see."

Accepting the small cold hand in order to help her down from the phaeton, he believed suddenly that she was terrified: her hand was trembling furiously.

Henry's muscles began to tense again, shoulders arched and calves taut and toes curled to the revolver, after the moment of weary peace he had known in the cold warming bed.

And again, though his body was warm under the blankets, even perspiring slightly, though his lungs still felt the heady sharp snowborn cold, he thought he was going to shiver. He remembered: she would not release his arm. She clutched at it with both small powerful hands like a frightened lemur, unspeaking, making no move toward the gate. At first he did not understand what she intended. Then, by the moonless starlight, he perceived she was not even looking at him. He turned to follow her glance between the stone gateposts, up the short drive whose dusty lambence was mottled and nearly devoured by weed growth, to the darker shape of the old boardinghouse. He understood that she was only pausing to think, to consider. And he knew without turning back to squint at her that she was shaken not by fear but in fevered anticipation. Anticipation of what? he thought. I've brought her out here and still I don't know. Then he thought: So I guess I am the one who deserves to be frightened. She said: "Do you have a pistol?"

"No'me," Henry said. "Miss Louisa, I don't think we should go up there. If you're worried about shooting I think we should just ride back to town and get the—"

"It could be anyone," she explained in a voice so uncharacteristically reasonable and dispassionate as to lack all conviction. She had only spoken, it seemed, to deny her own avid expectations and thereby perhaps quiet the shivering enough that she could begin walking. "We don't know."

Of course not, Henry said. "And it's private property. It doesn't even belong to us. So we should head back to town and tell the sheriff about what you think and then maybe he'll let us come back out here with him." She wasn't listening. She released her grip on him, took a step, and stumbled; he caught her.

"I'm afraid I will need your arm," she said. He heard her

breath, pulsing in short shallow nasal wheezes. She had to gather and swallow a deep gasp before she could speak again. "Come along." In the darkness, once more she spoke coyly: "Perhaps we will not require a pistol."

The drive seemed interminable. She labored along at his side, faltering over the weed-clumped and rutted dirt. The house rose like a full fat horizon moon, looming, swollen unnaturally on its bare hillside against the sky. It was a square graceless bulk, neither stately nor ominous, utilitarian, with halftoppled stone chimneys on each side like a pair of bookends. When they had reached the porch, it did not seem so huge. He guided her up the steps, supporting her from behind, almost lifting her by the elbows until she fled from his hands and was at the front door, trying the knob. The door was locked.

"You'll have to break it," she whispered.

"But—"

"Break it!" she hissed. "Kick it in. This house belonged to Uriah. It was stolen from him. I am his daughter, his only heir. Break it. Hurry." Henry twisted the knob and pushed. The door was solid.

"Listen, Miss Louisa," he said. "Why don't we—"

She turned from him and glided away. For an instant he thought she would storm back down the steps toward the phaeton. Following to the far end of the gallery, he found her before a window, trying to pry open the shutters with her fingernails.

"All right," Henry whispered, easing her aside. "All right."

The shutters were nailed. One side he pulled free without trouble; the other yielded to his force by breaking in half from the bottom. The sharp searing crack of dry wood was so loud that he stopped, startled, and listened beyond the fading report. She made a move to step by him. "Wait," he said.

A pane of the window was missing. He reached carefully through the shards to unlock the frame and then raised it, leaning forward into the room. Straining, head cocked to the left, he willed his hearing out through the musty dry darkness.

"All right," he repeated. "You go back to the door. I'll try to open it."

And then behind the front door, in the sightless void of the foyer, Henry had lingered, no longer or not for the moment afraid, before turning the latch. Just a foot away, beyond two inches of lumber, he heard or imagined he heard the shallow panting of Miss Louisa, waiting—as she had always waited: in patient implacable silence—for the door at last to be opened. His hand found the bolt's knob, but quietly, that she would not know for sure he was there, and he lingered. She has waited so long, he thought, remembering now in the Cambridge dark, with guilt and satisfaction, how he had paused, hand on the knob, extending her wait. Lucidly, he had stood wondering why it should be, how it had come to be, him, Henry Graham, of all mortals, who would finally unbolt this door and admit her. Lucidly, he had stood wondering whether the front room to the right of the hall, into which he had climbed and through which he had blindly groped, had perhaps once been the library.

She was holding a lighted candle, which illuminated her face starkly. It must have come, he thought to realize only later, and the match too, from some hiding-place in the black dress. She swept past him without speaking, bestowing only a swift yellow glance, perhaps in knowing reprimand for the delay. She had taken two steps up the stairway before she said anything, and then without turning, not in a whisper but in a loud full conversational steady voice:

"You will wait here."

Henry remembered vividly, palpably, the feeling of awestruck immobile impotence with which he had stood below watching the flickering candlelight advance, as though floating, up the stairs in her grasp. He watched her, above on the long balcony, brilliant and distant, like a lone actress spotlighted on stage. She moved deliberately to the door: knew where she was going, what she must do. She opened it gently and extended the candle before her.

"Chamberlain?"

Henry watched. Drawing back onto the balcony, she moved with the same resoluteness though less confidence, not so much as glancing toward Henry, this time perhaps out of pride, and chose another door, passing several, at the end of the landing. She disappeared beyond Henry's view; her candleglow was a dim indirect haze, reflected from gray bedroom walls through the narrow opening; her voice came again, loud and clear in the empty house.

"Chamberlain? Chamberlain?"

There was no scream. At first he only heard footsteps, then saw the dark figure gliding without a light across the upper hallway, reaching the stairs, and thought that she must be returning to him for assistance, for another match, and how she ought to slow down on the dark stairs or she would fall and cripple herself after having waited so long and come so far, and he nearly called out to her. But he did not. Then she passed him at the door still without slowing and gave him a look full in the face with eyes wide and unbelieving or beyond caring like a sleepwalker's, and went out, and he stood, knowing that he should and must follow her, now, at once, knowing equally that he could not. He remembered it all. He remembered thinking: What was it? Terror, fear? No, it has never been that. What then? Sorrow? Regret? Despair? Maybe pity? What then? and remembered too how he stood, frozen, thinking: But now I must see it too. Maybe I shouldn't.

Maybe my face will look like hers did, and I will never forget it. But I don't guess I'll ever forget even that face anyway now, so I might as well see. I might as well know. He remembered the stairs and the narrow balcony which he did not trust not to collapse and kill him and the door, which was ajar, which she had not in her exit bothered to close, which made no sound in the silent dry breathless air as he pushed it open and entered the bedroom.

Even without a candle, by now he could see well enough to discern that it was a figure, a body, in the bed. Against the dim gray rectangle of yellowed sheets he could make out in darker shades, darkened, almost as dark as a light Negro, the shape of arms, and hands folded prayerlike, and bony shoulders and bare sunken chest, and a head, hairless and shrunken and sharp-featured as an unfinished wooden marionette. Henry did not speak. He approached the bed. Leaning over it, unbreathing and unaware he was not breathing, he viewed the dried familiar aged unmistakable remains which Miss Louisa had recognized. He had seen no photographs, never so much as a cameo locket: but he knew before whose dusty catafalque he stood. Then the match cracked behind him like a pistol shot. And he turned, thinking already, lucidly, that if it were danger he would not have been warned with a match. He remembered it all.

—Who are you?

—I'm Henry Graham.

—Graham. Yes. I remember. Your paw rode beside Father during the War. They were with Earl Van Dorn.

—My grandfather. And you are—?

—Chamberlain Surrat.

—And this? You brought it back here—?

—Him. I brought him.

—To die?

—In his own house. Yes. To die.

—And it—him—and this was—?

—My father.

What he had seen, what he was told, and what he was left to imagine, all the twenty-eight years of troubled confused bitter exile and devotion, the years of waiting and hatred and resoluteness that twisted the soul like wind on a mountain-rock pine shrub, the news of Surrat's death and the final journey, out of Egypt, across unnamed and unnumbered flat corn-fat miles between Illinois and Kentucky, into Tennessee: Henry remembered.

—Your father?

—Yes. Uriah James.

—And the two of you—you came here—?

—No. He died on the way. In Tennessee. Two years ago.

—But you brought it—brought him on—?

—Here. To his own bed. Yes.

—And you are—?

—Chamberlain Surrat.

The chimes would ring again soon, any moment now, though for two o'clock or one-thirty or perhaps even one Henry could not recall, would not know until the sound came, if then: it seemed late. The room was silent, but for Ira's breathing, and very cold, tomblike, with a serious final compounded cold as though preparing for the dead profound moment of stillness before dawn.

—And this? What is this? What are you giving me?

—It was his. Uriah's. Take it.

—What is it?

—It's the proof. It's the letter.

—I don't want it.

—Take it.

"Of course," Ira said from the iron-cold darkness nearby.

"And why not?" Ira said. "They had gotten that far, crossed all the miles and years to Tennessee before the smallpox or brain fever or plain mortal expiration of anger-fed heart muscle caught up with Uriah, and it was what he most wanted, had waited for, so why not: Cham opened the old man like a catfish and gutted him out clean and then probably dried him on a rack of birch fencing in the nice hot Tennessee summer sun, like a piece of jerky. Maybe he even sewed him back up in front with a leather thong before the skin shrank too far, making a neat craftsmanlike job of it. And then hefted the thing back into the bed of their wagon, probably just where Uriah had died, only this time with a blanket all the way up over the head so folks wouldn't gawk on the road, and rolled on, skirting Hadrian, to install him in state for evermore to decrepitation on the throne of revenge: Uriah's own cuckolded marriage-bed. Where the old lady found him. It. But she never saw Cham, the lost love. So she waited the three months in simple astonishment or confusion before hiring the hearse to go back out there and claim what she knew was her father's body, if not how it had gotten there. Only Cham, sunken back over the years into some childlike pitiful simpering worshipful state of half-idiocy, did not understand: he thought they were coming to rob Uriah away from the only crypt in which he could ever know true rest. So he lit a second match. And this time it didn't burn down to his fingers while the two of you chatted."

Yes. Henry saw it, though he had not witnessed it: a flicker at that upstairs window, hardly more than a candlelight, as the hearse crawled awkwardly over the rutted and frozen drive, Miss Louisa leaning forward between the driver and the coroner, watching the window and so the first to cry out, not "It's on fire!" but merely "Faster. Can't you go faster?" and then within seconds the driver noticing too and stopping the hearse because flame had broken out, dancing up orange through the roof and in a few seconds more it was already too late. For a moment she stood peacefully between the two men watching those flames take the upper story and bearing against her face the steady unslackening blast of heat until suddenly she heard or thought she heard something above the sere crackling din or saw or thought she saw something at one of the windows, and she ran for the porch, shrieking Chamberlain's name. They had to stop her. She fought, and later the driver bore fingernail marks on his wrists and face. But there was nothing more they could do. By the time the coroner charged the porch and kicked open the door, the stairway was engulfed, and most of the lower hall. The draft from the open door merely hastened it. They restrained her and she continued to fight as the house before them seethed and brightened and then went foaming up in furious crimson and black and before very long dissolved to a shell. The only sounds resembling a human voice that either man heard were her wild cries, shrieking his name. Chamberlain. They saw no one. If a man, a living man, had been on the premises, he had either gotten out through the back, or was dead. Henry knew this: he had been told, in the fine slurred familiar hand of his father's letter:

—though even that is perhaps just another helpful optimistic assumption which we the living safely can neither confirm nor deny. Because who is to say that even the void which she entered to her seeming relief yesterday morning necessarily entails any final absence of pain? Not I. Perhaps void (or whatever we pretend to grasp, settle, tame by calling it with the word void) entails rather the absence of delusion or hope that there is, can ever be, final escape from pain. And perhaps in her particular inverted case these last thirty years were in fact the void out of which she has died, escaped, into some more fulfilling pain, or whatever. I will not say rest, peace (though I would have once, just as once, another and later time, I would have been equally sure that the void—which I so naively and devoutly believed I had tamed by the simple expedient of granting it untameability—did indeed entail absence even of pain, now I am not sure). Have I written that she failed to regain coherence? Perhaps even that is another crude solipsistic delusion of the living. She said she was going to Illinois. When they found her, pulled her drenched and all but frozen from that roadside slough up near Holly Springs, through the last hours of fever two nights ago and yesterday morning, she insisted upon it, I am told, over and over: she was going to Illinois. Well, perhaps she was. Perhaps she has. I for one will not say I know differently.

"So at the last she stopped waiting," Ira said. "She walked—how many?—almost thirty miles that day and night to catch up with Cham, to stop him before he fled the county in fear or despair or just satisfied terminal indifference (assuming that he was still alive, which was something she did have to assume) so she could tell him that it was all right, that those twenty-eight years had only been stolen from them. But thirty miles wasn't enough. Or (assuming he died with Uriah, I mean in the house, which for the sake of symmetry, closure, is the assumption I recommend) it was too much, and too late. But even if she had caught him, would it have mattered? Because the Chamberlain who had come back to that house believed Uriah, and believed *only* Uriah. And Uriah believed it was true, when Surrat had told Cham that he was Uriah's son. And the old lady only had Surrat's word otherwise, given five years ago, on a deathbed; which word Cham would not have accepted, not again, not a third time, after twenty-eight years of implacable hating equal to hers. And for that matter Uriah, judging from how he treated his daughter, would not have told Cham the truth if he knew it.

"So if Uriah believed or claimed to believe Cham was his son, but was a proven liar," Ira said, "and Surrat believed or claimed to believe Cham was his son, but he was a liar too, and the only person who could have known for sure if at all who had fathered Chamberlain was the fickle-hearted finishing-school girl-woman dead now some forty years, who probably did her own share of lying to both of them, then was it incest or not? Were they brother and sister, or not? Whose son *was* Chamberlain Surrat?"

In the iron-cold darkness, together, Ira and you wait for the reply.

Henry had grown weary. The revolver was warm at his feet, and he believed now he might sleep. He opened his eyes to the ceiling.

Yes, he thought, what is it that Father says: that man is born out of pain into helplessness and dies through pain into void and the best he can hope for is dispatch or postponement? Yes. So it is just the old withered meat after all, only that, defeated but unvanquished, desolated but evermore stubborn, and clinging from habit not even to the defeat or the desolation but to the very habit of clinging. She was going to Illinois, Henry thought. Despite all, after all, she was going to find him in Illinois. Well, maybe she has. Maybe she has. Who's to say differently, Henry thought.

"Correct," Henry said. "We don't even know that."

About the Author

David Quammen is a science journalist and essayist who began as a fiction writer. He has twice won the National Magazine award for his work in *Outside* magazine, where for fifteen years he was a natural-science columnist. He is the author of nine books, including three novels and this collection of stories. His nonfiction books include *The Song of the Dodo*, an exploration of global patterns in the evolution and extinction of species, which won the John Burroughs Medal and several other awards. Quammen has also received a Lannan Literary Fellowship and an Academy award from the American Academy of Arts and Letters. His most recent book is *The Boilerplate Rhino*, a collection of essays on human attitudes toward nature. He lives in Montana.